Edmund Yates

A Righted Wrong

Vol. III

Edmund Yates

A Righted Wrong
Vol. III

ISBN/EAN: 9783337053574

Printed in Europe, USA, Canada, Australia, Japan

Cover: Foto ©Andreas Hilbeck / pixelio.de

More available books at **www.hansebooks.com**

A RIGHTED WRONG.

A Novel.

BY

EDMUND YATES,

AUTHOR OF

'BLACK SHEEP,' 'THE FORLORN HOPE,' 'BROKEN TO HARNESS,' ETC.

IN THREE VOLUMES.

VOL. III.

LONDON:

TINSLEY BROTHERS, 18 CATHERINE ST., STRAND.

1870.

CONTENTS OF VOL. III.

A RIGHTED WRONG.

CHAPTER I.

TWENTY YEARS AFTER.

An unusually beautiful day, in an exceptionally beautiful summer, and a grand old mansion, in all its bravery, wearing its best air of preparation and festivity. Even in the merest outline such a picture has its charms; and that which the sunshine lighted up on one particular occasion, about to be described, merited close attention, and the study of its every detail.

Sheltered by a fine plantation, which, in any other than the land of flood and fell, might have been called a forest, and situated on the incline of a conical hill, the low park land, picturesquely planted, stretching away from it, until lost in the boundary of trees beneath,—a large, imposing house, built of gray, cut stone, presented its wide and lofty façade to the light. The architecture was irregular, picturesque, and effective; and now, with its numerous windows, some sparkling in the sunshine, others thrown wide open to admit the sweet air, the Deane had an almost palatial appearance. Along the front ran a wide stone terrace, from which three flights of steps, one in the centre, and one at either end, led down to an Italian garden, intersected by the wide avenue.

Large French windows opened on this stone expanse, and now, in the lazy summer day, the silken curtains were faintly stirring, and the sound of voices, and of occasional low laughter, came softly to the

hearing of two persons, a man and a woman, who were seated on a garden bench,
in an angle of the terrace. The countless
sounds of Nature, which make a music all
their own, were around them, and the
scene had in it every element of beauty
and joy; but these two persons seemed to
be but little moved by it, to have little in
common with all that surrounded them and
with the feelings it was calculated to suggest.

They were for the most part silent,
and when they spoke it was sadly and
slowly, as they speak upon whom the memory of the past is strong, and who habitually live in it more than in the present.
There was a deference in the tone and manner of the woman, which would have made
an observer aware that though the utmost
kindliness and unrestraint existed in her
relations with her companion, she was not
his equal in station; and her manner of

speaking, though quite free from all that ordinarily constitutes vulgarity, would have betrayed that difference still more plainly.

She was a tall woman, apparently about forty years old, and handsome, in a peculiar style. Her face was not refined, and yet far from common; the features well formed, and the expression eminently candid and sensible. Health and content were plainly to be read in the still bright complexion and clear gray Irish eyes. She wore a handsome silk dress, and a lace cap covered her still abundant dark hair, and in her dress and air were unmistakable indications of her position in life. She looked what she was, the responsible head of a household, authoritative and respected.

We have seen her before, many years ago, on board the ship which brought Margaret Hungerford to England, Margaret Hungerford, who has slept for nearly twenty years under the shade of the great

yew in the churchyard, which is not so
far from the Deane but that sharp eyes
can mark where the darker line of its solemn trees crosses the woods of the lower
park land. The years have set their mark
upon the handsome Irish girl, who had won
such trust and affection from the forlorn
young widow, who had done with it all
now, all love and fear, all sorrow and for-
lornness, and need of help, for ever. Not
only for ever, but so long ago, that her
name and memory were mere traditions,
while the trees she had planted were still
but youngsters among trees, and the path
cut through the Fir Field by her directions
was still known as the 'new' road.

There, on the spot where she had often
sat with Baldwin and talked of the future,
which they were never to see, Margaret's
friend, humble indeed, but rightly judged
and worthily trusted, sat, this beautiful

summer's day, in the untouched prime of
her health and strength and comeliness,
and talked of the dear dead woman; but
vaguely, timidly, as the long dead are
spoken of when they are mentioned at all
to one from whom the years had not ob-
scured her, though they had gathered the
dimness which age brings around every
other image of the past and of the future.

He with whom Rose Doran talked was
an old man, but older in mind and in health
than in years, of which he had not yet seen
the allotted number. Of a slight, spare
figure always, and now so bowed that the
malformation of the shoulders was merged
in the general bending weakness of the
frame, and the stooped head was habitually
held downwards, the old man might have
been of any age to which infirmity like his
could attain. Even on this warm day he
was wrapped in a cloak lined with fur,

and his white transparent face looked as
if warm blood had never coloured the fine
closely-wrinkled skin, on which the innumerable lines were marked as though they
had been cunningly drawn by needles. He
wore a low-crowned, wide-leaved soft hat,
and scanty silver locks showed under the
brim; but if the hat had been removed it
would have been seen that the head which
it had covered was almost entirely bald,
and of the same transparent ivory texture
as the face.

It would be difficult to imagine anything more fragile-looking than the old
man, as he sat, wrapped in his cloak, his
bowed shoulders supported by the angle
of the terrace, and his hands, long, white,
and skeleton-like, placidly folded on his
knees. The only trace of vigour remaining
in him was to be found in the eyes, and
here expression, feeling, memory yet lin-

gered, and sometimes gave forth such gleams
of light and purpose as seemed to tell of
the youth of the soul within him still.

A crutch stood against the wall by his
side, and a thick stick, with a strong ivory
handle, lay upon the bench. These were
unmistakable signs of the feebleness and
decay which had come to the old man, but
they would not have told a close observer
more than might have been learned by a
glance at his feet. They were not dis-
torted, none of the ugly shapelessness of
age and disease was to be seen there.
They were slim, and shapely, and neatly
attired, in the old-fashioned silk stocking
and buckled shoe of a more polite and
formal period, but they were totally inex-
pressive. No one could have looked at
the old man's feet, set comfortably upon
a soft lambskin rug, but remaining there
quite motionless, without seeing that they

had almost ceased to do their work. With much difficulty, and very slowly, by the aid of the crutch and the stick, they would still carry him a little way from the sunny sitting-room on the ground floor to the sunny corner of the terrace, for the most part—but that was all.

He was not discontented that it should be all, for he suffered little now in his old age—perhaps he had suffered as much as he could before that time came; and was no more irritable or peevish. A little tired, a little wondering betimes that he had so long to wait, while so many whose day had promised to be prolonged and bright in its morning had passed on, out of sight, before him: but a happy old man, for all that, in a quiet, musing way, and 'very little trouble to any one.'

Yes, that was the general opinion of Mr. Dugdale, old Mr. Dugdale, as the household, for some unexplained reason, called him, and few things vexed the spirit of Gertrude Baldwin so nearly beyond bearing, as the assurances to that effect which her aunt, Mrs. Carteret, was in the habit of promulgating to an inquisitive and sympathising neighbourhood. For Mrs. Carteret (she had been the eldest Miss Crofton a great many years ago) was not of a very refined nature, and it is just possible that when she commented on Mr. Dugdale's reduced and sometimes almost deathlike appearance, to the effect that any one ' to see him would think he could die off quite easily,' she rather resented his not availing himself of that apparent facility without delay. He did not, however; and Mrs. Carteret was the only person who ever found the gentle, kindly man in the way, and she never dared to hint to her husband that she did so.

Her niece inherited from her dead mother all the quick-sightedness which made
her keen to see and to suffer, where her
affections were concerned, and the first
seeds of dissension had been sown some
years before, between the aunt and the
niece, by the girl's perceiving that 'old'
Mr. Dugdale was not considered by Mrs.
Carteret as such an acquisition to the family
party at the Deane as its fair and gentle,
but high-spirited, young mistress held him
to be. It was on that occasion that Gertrude had contrived, very mildly and very
skilfully, but still after a decided and unmistakable fashion, to remind her aunt of
the fact that she, and not Mrs. Carteret,
was the lady of the house in which the old
man had been found *de trop;* and thence
had originated a state of things destined to
produce most unforeseen consequences.

The immediate result, however, had been

an increased observance in manner, and an
additional dislike in reality, to Mr. Dugdale, on the part of Mrs. Carteret, which
the old man perceived—as indeed he perceived everything, for his powers of observation were by no means enfeebled—but
which it never occurred to him to resent.
What could it possibly signify to him that
Mrs. Carteret did not like him, and wished
it might be in her power to get rid of him?
It was not in her power; it was not within
the compass of any earthly will to separate
him from Margaret's child ; and as for Mrs.
Carteret herself, it is to be feared that old
Mr. Dugdale, after the saturnine fashion of
his earlier years, cherished a quiet contempt
for that lady, while he readily acknowledged that she was a good sort of woman
in her way. It was not in his way, that
was all.

Mrs. Doran was especially devoted to

Mr. Dugdale, to whom she owed the prosperous position which she had held in the household at the Deane for so many years now, that she was as much a part of the place to the inhabitants as the forest trees or the family portraits. Consequently she was not particularly attached to Mrs. Carteret, and presumed occasionally to criticise that lady's proceedings after a fashion which, had she been aware of it, would have gone far to fortify her in one of her favourite and most frequently-expressed opinions, that it was a great mistake to keep servants too long. 'They always presume upon it, and become impertinent and troublesome.'

But Mrs. Carteret would never have ventured to include Mrs. Doran among the 'servants' otherwise than in her most private cogitations. Rose was a privileged person there, by a more sacred if not a

stronger right than that of Mrs. Carteret
herself.

But on this bright, beautiful day, when
the old man had come out upon the terrace to bask awhile in the genial sunshine,
why was Rose Doran with him? Ordinarily he had younger, fairer companions, in
whose faces and voices there were many
happy, sad memories for him, and whose
love and care brightened the days fast
going down to the last setting of the sun
of his life. They were absent to-day, and
the two to whom, of all the numerous
household at the Deane, the day had most
of retrospective meaning were alone together.

'It's wonderful how well I remember
her, sir,' Rose was saying; 'sometimes that
is. There's many a day I disremember her
entirely, but when I do think about her—
as to-day—I can see her plain. And I'm

glad, somehow, I never saw her in her grandeur; for if I did, an' all the years that have gone by since then, I couldn't but think no one else had a right to it.'

'I understand what you mean, Rose, and when I remember her, sometimes, as you say, it isn't in her grandeur, but as she was when you and she came home first.'

'Yes, sir, and you saw us goin' in at the door of the little inn—who'd ever think there'd be a hotel as big as Morrison's, and a deal cleaner, in the very same place now? —and you not knowin' us, and she seein' you in a minute. Isn't it strange, Mr. Dugdale, to remember it after twenty, ay, more than twenty years? How long is it then, sir, rightly?'

'Twenty-three years and some months, Rose.'

'True for you, sir. And now Miss

Gerty's to be her own mistress, and no one
to say by your leave or with your leave to
her, the darling! The master would have
been a proud man, rest his soul! this
day.'

The old man did not notice her remark.
But after a little while, as if he had been
thinking over it, he bowed the bent head
still lower, and moved the thin white hands,
and sighed.

'Are you chilly at all, sir?' asked his
quickly-observant companion. 'The sun is
shifting a little; would you like to go in?'

'No,' he replied; and then asked, after
a pause, 'How are they getting on?'

'Beautifully,' Rose answered. 'The
house is a picture; and as to the ball-room,
nothing could be more beautiful. Miss
Eleanor has it all done out with flowers,
and I'm only afraid she'll be tired before
the time comes for the dancing. Do you

think you'll be able to sit up to see it, sir?'

'I don't know, Rose; but I will try. Gerty seems to wish it so much, foolish child; as if it could make any difference to her that an old man like me should be there to see her happy and admired.'

'An' why shouldn't she?' remonstrated Rose in a tone almost of vexation. 'Do you think the children oughtn't to have some nature in them? If Miss Gerty was no better nor a baby when the mistress— the Lord be good to her!—was taken, and Miss Eleanor never saw the smile of her mother's face at all, sure they know about her all the same, and it's more and not less they think about her, the older they grow, and the better they know the want of a mother, through seeing other people with mothers and fathers and friends of all kinds, and no one to dare to deny them—

not that I'm sayin' or thinkin' there's any
one would harm innocent lambs like them,
nor try to put between them — but the
world's a quare world, Mr. Dugdale, and
they're beginnin' to find it out, and the
more they know of it, the more they miss
the mother they never knew at all, and the
father they did not know much about—and
the more they cling to them that did know,
and can tell them.   Many's the time, Mr.
Dugdale, that Miss Gerty has said to me,
" Isn't it odd that uncle James remembers
mamma much better than uncle Carteret or
aunt Lucy remember her, and can tell us
much more about our father?—and yet they
were all young people together, and near
relations, and he wasn't."   And it was only
the other day, when you told Miss Gerty she
was to have the poor mistress's picture for
her comin' of age, she says to me, " There's
uncle and aunt Carteret couldn't tell me

whether it's like her or not; and there's uncle James knows all about it, and can tell when I'm like her and when Nelly is, and yet they say old people forget everything." Beggin' your pardon, sir, for saying you're old, but the dear child said the very words. An' so, if she didn't want you to-night to see her in her glory, and to be like the smile of the father and mother that's in heaven upon her, I wouldn't think much of her, Mr. Dugdale, 'deed I wouldn't then.'

'Well, well, Rose, it seems the children are of your opinion, for they have made me promise to sit up as late as possible; and I have heard as much about their dresses as either their maids or yourself, I'll be bound.'

'An' beautiful they'll look in them, Mr. Dugdale, particularly Miss Gerty. Don't you think she grows wonderfully like her mother? Not that I ever saw her look bright and happy like Miss Gerty; but I think she must have been just like her, after she was married to the poor master. You know I went away before that, sir; but perhaps you disremember.'

'No, no, Rose, I remember. I remember it all very well, because she told me if she wanted you and could not send for you herself I was to do so, because Mr. Baldwin did not know you. No, no; it is a long time ago, a very long time, but I don't forget, I don't forget.'

'An' you see the likeness, sir?'

'Yes, I see the likeness, I see it very plainly; as we grow old, time seems so much shorter that it does not appear at all strange to me that I should remember her so well. There were many years during which I could hardly recall her face even when I was looking at the picture, but all that dimness seems to have cleared away now, and all my memory come back. Gerty is wonderfully like her, only more placid; her manner is more like her father's.'

They were silent for a time, during which Rose Doran knitted diligently,—her fingers were never idle, and her subordinates in the household said the same of her eyes and ears,—and then she began to talk again.

'It'll be a fine ball, sir. They say the beautifulest, except the Duke's, that ever was in this part of the country. And sure, so it ought, for where's there the like of Miss Baldwin of the Deane for beauty or for fortune either? An' what could be too good in the way of a ball for *her?*'

There was a note of challenge in the Irishwoman's voice. Mr. Dugdale observed it with amusement, and replied,

'I daresay it will go off very well. Mrs.

Carteret is a good hand at this kind of thing.'

'She is,' said Rose shortly; 'and as it's Miss Gerty's money it's all to come out of, she'll have no notion of saving anything.'

This was the nearest approach to a frank expression of her not-particularly-exalted opinion of Mrs. Carteret on which Rose had ever ventured, and Mr. Dugdale did not encourage her to pursue it by any remark; but, observing that the girls had said they would come out to him, and were after their time, and that he would go and look for them, he began to make slow preparations for a change of place.

Rose's steady arm aided him, and he was soon proceeding slowly along the terrace, his crutch under his left arm and his stick in his right hand, while Rose walked by his side. As he slowly and apparently painfully dragged himself along—only apparently, for he rarely suffered pain now —Mr. Dugdale presented a picture of decrepitude which contrasted strangely with a picture which any observer, had there chanced to be one upon the terrace that day, might have seen, and which he and Rose stood still to look at with intense pleasure.

Through the open windows of a large room upon the terrace the interior was to be seen. The apartment was of splendid dimensions, and the richly-decorated walls and ceiling were ornamented with classical designs appropriate to the festive purposes of a ball-room. A bank of flowers was constructed to enclose a space designed for an orchestra, and several musical instruments were already arranged in their places.

A grand piano was in the middle, and a lady was seated before it, whose nimble fingers were flying over the keys, producing the strains of a brilliantly provocative and inspiriting valse. The lady was not alone. In the centre of the room, whose polished floor was almost as bright and slippery as glass, stood two young girls, the arms of each around the waist of the other, their heads thrown back, their eyes beaming with laughter, and their hearts beating with the exertion of the wild dance they had just concluded.

As Mr. Dugdale and Rose drew near the window, the pause for breath came to a conclusion, the music gushed forth, more than ever inviting, and the dancers were off again, spinning round and round in their girlish glee in a boisterous exaggeration of the figure of the dance, irresistibly merry and attractive. They flew down the length of the room, crossed to its extremity, and came whirling up to the central window.

There stood Mr. Dugdale with uplifted threatening stick, and Rose, with her knitting dropped, fascinated with admiration. Then they checked their headlong career, and, with some difficulty, came to a stop opposite the pair on the terrace, laughingly shaking their heads in imitation of the pretended rebuke they were conveying.

'A rational way to rehearse for your ball, Gerty,' said Mr. Dugdale, as he stepped, with the assistance of the young girl's ready hand, into the room, followed by Rose. 'And a capital plan for you, Nelly, who are so easily tired. You silly children, don't you think you will have enough dancing to-night?'

'Not half enough,' replied one of the girls, 'not quarter; none of the people will stay after five or six at the latest.'

'I should hope not, indeed,' said Mr. Dugdale. 'And you are resolved to begin punctually at ten; you *are* unconscionable.'

'And then you know, uncle James,' said the girl whom he had called Gerty, 'we cannot dance together to-night; we are grown up, you know, hopelessly grown up; it's awful, isn't it? and besides·—besides aunt Lucy tempted us with her beautiful playing—and the floor is so delightful; and now don't you really, really think it will be a delightful ball?'

'I have not the smallest misgiving about it, Gerty, though I don't know much of balls. But I am sure Mrs. Carteret will join me in urging you not to tire yourselves any more just now.'

Mrs. Carteret left the piano, and joined the girls, who immediately entered on a discussion of the measures already taken for the beautification of the ball-room, and the possibility of still farther adorning it, which was finally pronounced hopeless, everything being already quite perfect, and the party adjourned to luncheon.

So the years had sped away, and all the fears, and hopes, and sorrows they had given birth to had also come to their death, according to the wonderful law of immutability, and were no more. The mother in her marble tomb beneath the yew-tree, the father in his unmarked grave in the desert, but united in the country too far off for mortal ken or comprehension, were well-nigh forgotten here; and their children were women now.

The little party assembled at the Deane on this occasion — the twenty-first anniversary of Gertrude Baldwin's birth — had but little sadness among them, and were visited with but slight recollections of the far distant past. Twenty years is a long

time. No saying can be more trite and
more true; yet there are persons and circumstances, and, more than all, there are
feelings which are not forgotten, ignored,
killed in twenty years.

There were two unseen guests that day
at the table—at whose head Mrs. Carteret,
who was in a gracious, not to say gushing
mood, insisted on Gertrude's taking her
place for the first time—whose presence
Mr. Dugdale felt, though he was an old
man now, and his fancy was no longer
active. He had his place opposite to Gertrude, and from it he could see, hanging on
the wall behind her chair, her father's portrait. It was a fine picture, the work of a
first-rate artist, and the face was full of
harmony and expression. The graceful
lines, the rich colouring of youthful manhood were there, and the sunny blue eyes
smiled as if they could see the gay girls,

the handsome, self-conscious, self-important woman, the wan and feeble old man. From the portrait Mr. Dugdale's glance wandered to the girlish face and figure before him and just under it; and a pang of exceeding keen and bitter remembrance smote him—ay, after twenty years.

Gertrude Meriton Baldwin was a handsomer girl than her mother had been, but wonderfully like her. No trouble, no care, no touch of degradation, humiliation, concealment, bitterness of any kind, had ever lighted on the daughter's well-cared-for girlhood, which had been permitted all its natural expansion, all its legitimate enjoyment and careless gladness. No passion, unwise and ungoverned, had come into her life to trouble and disturb it too soon—to fill it with vain illusions, and the sure heritage of disappointment. A happy childhood had grown into a happy girlhood, and now that happy girlhood had ripened into a womanhood, with every promise of happiness for the future.

She was taller than her mother, and had more colour; but the features were almost the same. The brow was a little less broad, the lips were fuller, but the eyes were in no way different, so far as they had been called upon for expression up to the present time; they had looked like Margaret's, and no doubt would so look in every farther development of life, circumstance, and character.

Eleanor, who amused herself during the luncheon,—at which Mr. Dugdale was unusually silent, and Mrs. Carteret occupied herself rather emphatically, on the plea that dinner was a doubtful good when a ball was in preparation,—was not in the least like her father, her mother, or her sister. She was very small, delicately formed, and fragile in appearance, with a clear dark complexion, large black eyes, and a profusion of glossy black hair, which, especially when in close contrast with the clear gray eyes and soft brown hair of her sister, gave her a foreign appearance, of which she was quite conscious and rather proud.

Hitherto there had been no difference in the lot of the sisters. The childish joys and sorrows of the one had been those of the other, and girlhood had brought to them no separate fortune. Nor were things materially altered now. The independence of action which Gertrude attained upon this day would be Eleanor's in a very short time, and in point of wealth they were nearly equal. For each there had been a long minority. Eleanor Davyntry had not long survived her brother, and all her disposable fortune was her younger niece's Apart from their orphanhood, no girls

could have had a more enviable lot than
the two who were in such wild spirits on
that summer's day, which invested one of
them with all the dignity of legal woman-
hood, and all the responsibility of a great
heiress.

Eleanor was of a different temperament
from that of Gertrude, more vehement,
more passionate, less self-reliant, less sustained. Hitherto the difference had shown itself but seldom and slightly, and there had
been little or nothing to develop it. But
a shrewd observer would have noticed it,
even in the manner in which each regarded
the promised pleasure of the evening, in
the easy joyousness of the one, and the
passionate eagerness of the other.

When luncheon had nearly reached a
conclusion, the sounds of wheels upon the
drive sent Eleanor rushing to the window.
A stylish dog-cart, in which were seated a

tall, fine-looking, rather heavy middle-aged man and an irreproachable groom, was rapidly approaching the house.

'It is uncle,' said Eleanor; 'now we shall know for certain who's coming from Edinburgh. What a good thing you thought of the telegraph, aunt!'

'Yes,' said Mrs. Carteret. 'When one has to put people up for the night, it is better to know exactly how many to expect.'

In a few minutes Haldane Carteret was in the room, and had handed an open telegraphic despatch to Gertrude.

'They're all coming, you see,' he said good-humouredly; 'and *you'll* be glad to hear, Lucy, there's no doubt about Meredith. He has got that troublesome business settled, as he always does get everything settled he puts his mind to, and he will be down by the mail, and here by eleven.'

' That *is* delightful,' said Gertrude,
with frank outspoken pleasure. 'You have
brought nothing but good news, uncle.'

' And the programmes—isn't that what
you call them? I hope they're all right.'

' I'm sure they are.—Aunt, what room
are you going to give Mr. Meredith?'

Then ensued a domestic discussion, in
which Gertrude and Mrs. Carteret took an
active share; but Eleanor stood looking out
of the window, and did not utter a word.

CHAPTER II.

ROBERT MEREDITH.

THE twenty years which had rolled over the head of Robert Meredith, the anxiously expected guest, since last we saw him, may be thus briefly recapitulated. The school selected by James Dugdale for his protégé's education was the now celebrated, but then little heard-of Grammar-school of Lowebarre. Not that the *alumni*, as they delight to call themselves, recognise their old place of education by any such familiar name. To them it is and always will be the Fairfax-school; they are 'Fairfaxians,' and the word Lowebarre is altogether ignored.

The *fons et origo* of these academic groves, pleasantly situate in the immediate vicinity of the metropolis, was one Sir Anthony Fairfax, a worthy knight of the time of Queen Elizabeth, who, having lived his life merrily, according to the fashion of the old English gentlemen of those days, more especially in the matter of the consumption of sack and the carrying out of the *droits de seigneurie*, thought it better towards his latter days to endeavour to get up a few entries on the other side of the ledger of his life, and found the easiest method in the doing a deed of beneficence on a large scale. This was nothing less than the foundation of a school at Lowebarre, where a portion of his property was situate, for the education of forty boys, who were to be gratuitously instructed in the learned languages, and morally and religiously brought up. How the scheme worked in those dark ages it is, of course, impossible to say.

But ten years before Robert Meredith was inducted into the *arcana* of the classics the Fairfax school was in a very low state indeed, and the Fairfaxians themselves were no better than a set of roughs. The head master, an old gentleman who had been classically educated, indeed, but over whose head the rust of many years of farming had accumulated, took little heed of his scholars, whose numbers consequently dwindled half-year by half-year, and who, as they neglected not only the arts but everything else but stone-throwing and orchard-robbing, had no manners to soften, and became brutal.

This state of affairs could not last. One of the governors or trustees acting under the founder's will saw that not merely was the muster-roll of the school diminishing, but its social *status* was almost gone. He called a meeting of his coadjutors, impressed upon them the necessity of taking vigorous steps for getting rid of the then head master, and of at once procuring the services of a man ready to go with the times. Advertisements judiciously worded were sent to all the newspapers, inviting candidates for the head-mastership of the Fairfax school, and dilating in glowing terms on the advantages of that position; but time passed, and the post yet remained open. Those who presented themselves were too much of the stamp of the existing holder of the situation to suit the enlarged views of the trustees, and it was not until Mr. Warwick, the governor who had first suggested the reform, busied himself personally in the matter, that the fitting individual was secured.

The Rev. Charles Crampton, who, having taken a first-class in classics and a

second in mathematics, having been Fellow
of his college and tutor of some of the best
men of their years, had finally succumbed
to the power of love, and subsided into a
curacy of seventy - five pounds a year, was
Mr. Warwick's selection. He brought with
him testimonials of the highest character;
but what weighed most with Mr. Warwick
was the earnest recommendation of James
Dugdale, who had been Mr. Crampton's
college friend.

Poor Charles Crampton, when he sacri-
ficed his fellowship for love, had little
notion that he would have to pass the
remainder of his life in grinding in a mill
of boys. To study the Fathers, to prepare
two or three editions of his favourite classic
authors, to play in a more modern and refined manner the part of the parson in the
'Deserted Village,' had been his hope.
But though the old adage was not followed,

though when Poverty came in at the door
(and she did come speedily enough, not in
her harshest fiercest aspect it is true, but
looking quite grimly enough to frighten an
educated and refined gentleman), Love did
not fly out of the window, yet Charles
Crampton had suffered sufficiently from
turpis egestas to induce him at once to
accept the offer.

The salary of the Fairfax head-mastership, though not large, quintupled his then
income; the position held out to him was
that of a gentleman, and though he had not
any wild ideas of the dignity and responsibility of a school-mastership, the notion of
having to battle in aid of a failing cause
pleased and invigorated him, more especially
when he reflected that, should he succeed,
the *kudos* of that success would be all his
own.

So the Reverend Charles Crampton was

installed at Lowebarre, and the wisdom of Mr. Warwick's selection was speedily proved. Men of position and influence in the world, who had been Mr. Crampton's friends at college; others, a little younger, to whom he had been tutor; and the neighbouring gentry, when they found they had resident among them one who was not merely a scholar and a man of parts, but by birth and breeding one of themselves,— sent their sons to the Fairfax school, and received Mr. and Mrs. Crampton with all politeness and attention.

By the time that Robert Meredith arrived at Lowebarre the school was thoroughly well known; its scholars numbered nearly two hundred; its 'speechdays' were attended, as the local journals happily expressed it, 'by lords spiritual and temporal, the dignitaries of the Bar, the Bench, and the Senate, and the flower of

the aristocracy;' while, source of Mr. Crampton's greatest pride, there stood on either
side of the Gothic window in the great
school-hall, on a chocolate ground, in gold
letters, a list of the exhibitioners of the
school, and of the honours gained by Fairfaxians, at the two universities.

To a boy brought up amidst the incon-
gruities of colonial life the order and regularity of the Fairfax school possessed all
the elements of bewildering novelty. But
with his habitual quietude and secret observation Robert Meredith set himself to
work to acquire an insight into the charac-
ters both of his masters and his school-fel-
lows, and determined, according to his wont,
to turn the result of his studies to his own
benefit.

The forty boys provided for by the
beneficence of good old Sir Anthony Fairfax—'foundation-boys,' as they were called

—were now, of course, in a considerable minority in the school. They were for the most part sons of residents in the immediate neighbourhood; but for the benefit of those young gentlemen who came from afar, the head master received boarders at his own house, and at another under his immediate control, while certain of the under masters enjoyed similar privileges.

The number of young gentlemen received under Mr. Crampton's own roof was rigidly limited to three; for Mrs. Crampton was a nervous little woman, who shrunk from the sound of cantering bluchers, and whose housekeeping talent was not of an extensive order. The triumvirate paid highly, more highly than James Dugdale thought necessary; and Hayes Meredith was of his opinion. The boy would have to rough it in after life, he said,—'roughing it' was a traditional idea with him,—

and it would be useless to bring the lad up
on velvet. So that Robert found his quar-
ters in Mr. Crampton's second boarding-
house, where forty or fifty lads, all the sons
of gentlemen of modern fortune, dwelt in
more or less harmony out of school-hours,
and were presided over by Mr. Boldero,
the mathematical master.

On his first entry into this herd of boys,
Robert Meredith felt that he could scarcely
congratulate himself on his lines having
fallen in pleasant places. He had sufficient
acuteness to foresee what the lively youths
amongst whom he was about to dwell
would reckon as his deficiencies, and consequently would select and enter upon at
once to his immediate opprobrium. That
he was colonial, and not English born,
would be, he was aware, immediately resented with scorn by his companions, and
regarded as a reason for overwhelming him

with obloquy. It was, therefore, a fact to be kept most secret; but after the lapse of a few days it was inadvertently revealed by the 'chum' to whom alone Robert had mentioned the circumstance. When once known it afforded subject for the keenest sarcasm; ' bushranger,' ' kangaroo,' ' ticket-of-leave,' were among the choice epithets bestowed upon him.

It would not be either pleasant or profitable to linger over the story of Robert Meredith's school-days. They have no interest for us beyond this, that they developed his disposition, and insensibly influenced all his after life. He regarded his schoolmates with scorn as unbounded as it was studiously concealed, and he cultivated their unsuspecting good-will with a success which rendered him in a short time, in all points essential to his comfort, their master. He made rapid progress in his studies, and kept before his mind with steadiness which was certainly wonderful at his age—and, had it been induced by a more elevated actuating motive, would have been most admirable—the purpose with which he had come to England.

When the end of his schoolboy life drew near, and the much longed-for University career was about to begin, Robert Meredith took leave of Mr. Crampton with mutual assurances of good-will. If the conscientious and reverend gentleman had been closely questioned with regard to his sentiments concerning his clever colonial pupil, he must have acknowledged that he admired rather than liked him. But there was no one to dive into the secrets of his soul, and in the letter which Mr. Crampton addressed to Mr. Dugdale on the occasion, he gave him, with perfect truth, a highly favourable account of Robert Meredith, of which one sentence really contained the pith. 'He is conspicuous for talent,' wrote the reverend gentleman; 'but I think even his abilities are less marked than his tact, in which he surpasses any young man whose character has come under my observation.'

'So in argument, and so in life—tact is a great matter.' Behold the guiding spirit of Robert Meredith's career, even in its present fledgling days. It was tact that made him eschew anything that might look like 'sapping,' or rigidity of morals, as much as he eschewed dissipation and actual fast life while at college. It was tact that made his wine-parties, though the numbers invited were small, and the liquids by no means so expensive as those furnished by many of his acquaintances, the pleasantest in the university. It was tact that took him now and then into the hunting-field, that made him a constant attendant at Bullingdon and Cowley Marsh, where his bowling and batting rendered him a welcome ally and a formidable opponent ; and it was tact which allotted him just that amount of work necessary for a fair start in his future career.

Robert Meredith knew perfectly that in that future career at the bar the honours gained at college would have little weight —that the position to be gained would depend materially upon the talent and industry brought to bear upon the dry study of the law itself, upon the mastery of technical details ; above all, upon the reading of that greatest of problems, the human heart, and the motives influencing it. To hold his own was all he aimed at while at college, and he did so ; but some of his friends, who knew what really lay in him, were grievously disappointed when the lists

were published, and it was found that Robert Meredith had only gained a double
second. George Ritherdon grieved openly,
and refused to be comforted even by his
own success, and by the acclamations which
rang round the steady reading set of Bod-
hamites when it was known that George
Ritherdon's name stood at the head of the
first class.

The two friends were not to be sepa-
rated—that was Ritherdon's greatest consolation. Mr. Plowden, the great convey-
ancer of the Middle Temple, had made
arrangements to receive both of them to
read with him; and in the very dingy
chambers occupied by that great professor
of the law they speedily found themselves
installed. A man overgrown with legal
rust, and prematurely drowsy with a life-
long residence within the 'dusty purlieus
of the law,' was Mr. Plowden; but his

name was well known, his fame was thoroughly established; many of his pupils were leading men at the bar; and the dry tomes which bore his name as author were recognised text-books of the profession.

Moreover, James Dugdale had heard, from certain old college chums, that underneath Mr. Plowden's legal crust there was to be found a keen knowledge of human nature, and a certain power of will, which, properly exercised, would be of the greatest assistance in moulding and forming such a character as Robert Meredith's. It was, therefore, with a comfortable sense of duty done that James Dugdale saw the young man established in Mr. Plowden's chambers, and, from all he had heard, he was by no means sorry that Robert was to have George Ritherdon as his companion.

There are certain persons who seem to be specially designed and cut out by nature for prosperity, and with whom, on the whole, it does not seem to disagree. They bear the test well, they are not arrogant, insolent, or apparently unfeeling, and they make more friends than enemies. Such people find many true believers in them, to surround them with a sincere and heartfelt worship, to regard all their good fortune as their indisputable right, and resent any cross, crook, or turning in it as an injustice on the part of Providence, or 'some one.' We all know one person at least of this class, for whose 'luck' it is difficult to account, except as 'luck,' and of whom no one has anything unfavourable to say, or the disposition to say it.

Robert Meredith was one of this favoured class of persons. He had the good fortune to possess certain external gifts which go far towards making a man popular, and under which it is always difficult, especially to women, to believe that a cold heart is concealed. The handsome lad had grown up into a handsomer man, and one chiefly remarkable for his easy and graceful manners, which harmonised with an elegant figure and a voice which had a very deceptive depth, sweetness, and impressiveness of intonation about it.

The ardent admirer, the unswerving true believer in Meredith's case was, as we have seen, George Ritherdon; and it would have been curious and interesting to investigate the extent and importance of the influence of this early contracted and steadily maintained friendship on the lives of both men, and on the estimation in which Meredith was held by the world outside that companionship.

He would have been very loth to believe that any particle of his importance, a shade of warmth in the manner of his welcome

anywhere, an impulse of confidence in his
ability, leading to his being employed in
cases above his apparent mark and standing, were the result of an unexpressed belief in George Ritherdon, a tacit but very
general respect and admiration for the earnest, honest, irreproachable integrity of the
man, who was clever, indeed, as well as
good, but so much more exceptionally good
than exceptionally clever, that the latter
quality was almost overlooked by his
friends, who were numerous and influen-
tial. Wherever George's influence could
reach, wherever his efforts could be made
available, Meredith's interests were safe,
Meredith's ambition was aided.

Naturally of a frank and communicative
disposition, liking sympathy and the expression of it, fond of his home and his
family, and ever ready to be actively interested in all that concerned them, there

was not an incident in his history, direct
or indirect, with which he would not have
made his 'chum' acquainted on the least
hint of the 'chum's' desiring to know it;
and, in fact, Robert Meredith, who had too
much tact to permit his friend to perceive
that his communicativeness occasionally
bored him, was in thorough possession of
his friend's history past and present.

But this was not reciprocal, except in
a very superficial scale. Robert Meredith
was perhaps not intentionally reticent with
George Ritherdon, and it occurred very seldom to the latter to think his friend reticent
at all, but he was habitually cautious. The
same quality which had made him a taciturn
observer in the house at Chayleigh, able to
conceal his dislike of Mr. Baldwin, and to
appreciate thoroughly without appearing
to observe the tie which bound James Dugdale to his old friend's daughter, now in

his manhood enabled him to win the regard of others, and to learn all about them,
without letting them either find out much
about him, or offending them, or inspiring
them with distrust by cold and calculated
reserve.

As a matter of fact, George Ritherdon
knew very much less of his friend than his
friend knew of him, and of one portion of
his life he was in absolute ignorance. It
was that which included his residence at
Chayleigh, and his subsequent relations
with the families of Carteret and Baldwin.
George had heard the names in casual
mention, and he knew that when Meredith
went for a fortnight or so to Scotland in the
'long' he went to a place called the Deane,
where a retired officer of artillery, named
Haldane Carteret, lived, who kept a very
good house, and gave 'men' some very
capital shooting.

But George did not shoot; and had he been devoted to that manly pursuit, he would never have thought it in the least unkind or negligent in Meredith to have omitted to share his opportunities in that way with him; he would never have thought about it at all indeed; so the Deane was quite unknown territory, even speculatively, to this good fellow. He knew nothing of the young heiress and her sister. No stray photograph or missish letter, left about in the careless disarray of bachelor's chambers, had ever excited George's curiosity, or led to 'chaff' on his part upon Meredith's predilection for travelling north, whenever he could spare the time to travel at all, upon his indifference to 'the palms and temples of the south.' George was not an adept in the polite modern art of 'chaff,' and few men could have been found to offer less occasion for its exercise than Robert Meredith.

It had sometimes occurred to George to wonder why a man so popular with women, so 'rising' as Robert Meredith, a man who had undoubtedly, in default of some untoward accident, a brilliant professional career and all its concomitant social advantages before him, had not married; but this was a matter on which he would not have considered that even their close friendship would have justified him in putting any questions to Meredith.

The *tu quoque* which might have been Meredith's reply was of easy explanation. George Ritherdon had had a disappointment in his youth, and had never thought seriously about marriage since. The disappointment had taken place in his early imprudent days, when no connection, even distantly collateral, existed in his mind between money and marriage, and he had long since arrived at the conviction that, even if it did come into his head or heart to fall in love again, he could not afford to marry, and therefore must, acting upon the gentlemanly precepts which had always governed him, resist any such inclination as dishonourable to himself and ungenerous towards its object.

The world had 'marched' to a very quick step indeed since the days of George's almost boyhood, when the beautiful but penniless Camilla Jackson had fascinated him 'into fits' at a carpet dance in the neighbourhood of his father's house, and he had forthwith set to work, in the fervent realms of his imagination, to fit up, furnish, and start a most desirable and charming little establishment, to be presided over by that young lady in the delightful capacity of wife. Of course the beautiful Camilla was always to be attired in the choicest French millinery and the clearest white muslins. Laundresses' bills had no place, nor had those of the *modiste*, in the unsophisticated imagination of the young man, and breakages were as far from his thoughts as babies.

George had lived and learned since then, and he dreamed no more dreams now; he knew better. Unless some tremendous, wholly unexpected, and extravagantly-unlikely piece of good luck should come in his way—something about as probable as the adventures of Sindbad or Prince Camaralzaman, in which case he would immediately look about for an eligible young lady to take the larger share of it off his unaccustomed hands—George would now never marry.

Camilla had disdained the white muslin and the millinery regardless of the washing bill, of which indeed she had early been taught by an exemplary and fearfully managing mother to be ceaselessly reminiscent; and George not unfrequently saw her now in a carriage, the mere varnish whereof told of wealth of perfectly aggressive amount, in a carriage crammed with healthy, clean, rich-looking children, and gorgeously arrayed in velvets and furs of great price.

That Meredith was not a marrying man was the conclusion at which George Ritherdon arrived, when he discussed with himself the oddity of the coincidence which threw them together, and speculated upon how long the engagement would last.

In one respect the friends were very differently circumstanced. George Ritherdon had 'no end' of relations, cousins by the score, aunts and uncles in liberal proportions. But Robert Meredith was a lonely man. His colonial origin explained that. He had never sought to renew any of the ties of family connection broken by his

father when he left England ; he had found
friends steady and serviceable, and he wisely
preferred contenting himself with them to
cultivating dubiously disposed relatives.
Boy though he was, he made a correct hit
in this.

'If they were likely to be any use to
me, my father would have put me in some
kind of communication with them ; he certainly would have looked them up when he
came home, which he never did.'

Therefore Robert never troubled himself more about any of the family connections on this side of the world, and, indeed,
troubled himself very little about those on
the other. As time went by he was accustomed to say to himself that he knew they
were all getting on well, and that was
enough for him. Sometimes he wondered
whether he should ever see them again ;
whether, if he did not 'see his way' here,

he might not go in for colonial practice;
whether one or more of his brothers, children when he saw them last, might not
take the same fancy which he had taken
for seeing the old world. But nothing of
all this happened.

Robert Meredith had neared the end of
his college career when intelligence of his
father's death reached him, and caused
him genuine, if temporary, suffering. His
thoughts went back then to the old home
and the old times, and he did feel for a
time a disinterested wish that he had been
with his mother—how she had loved him,
how she loved him still, through all those
years of separation ! — when this calamity
came upon her. The necessity for a
large correspondence with his brothers, and
the feeling, always a terrible one in cases
where a long distance lies between persons
affected by the same event, that his father's

death had taken place while he was quite unconscious of it, and was already long past when he heard of it, touched chords dulled if not silenced.

The account which he received of family affairs was prosperous : one of his sisters was already married, the other would follow her example after a due and decorous lapse of time. His brothers were to carry on Hayes Meredith's business, in whose profits his father left him a small share. Altogether, apart from feeling—and it was unusual for Robert Meredith to find it difficult to keep any matter of consideration apart from feeling—the position of affairs was eminently satisfactory, and the young man, ambitious, industrious, and self-reliant, felt that he and his were well treated by fate.

He felt the blank which his father's death created a good deal. He had corresponded with him very regularly, and the freshness and vigour, the plain practical sense and shrewdness of the older man's mind had been pleasant and useful to the younger. He had not expected the event, either. Hayes Meredith was a strong, hale, athletic man, and his son had always thought of him as he had last seen him. No bad accounts of his health had ever reached Robert, and he had never thought of his father's death as a probable occurrence.

On the whole, this was the most remarkable event, and by many degrees the most impressive, which had befallen in Meredith's life, and its influence upon him was decidedly injurious. He had always been hard, and from that time he became harder —not in appearance, nothing was more characteristic of the young man than his easy and sympathetic manner, but in reality he felt more solitary now that the one bond of intellectual companionship between him and his home was broken, and this solitude was not good for him. As for his mother, he was apt to think of her as a very good woman in her way—an excellent woman indeed. A man must be much worse than Robert Meredith before he ceases to believe this of his own mother; but she knew nothing whatever of the world—of the old world particularly—and could not be made to understand it. He wrote to her—he never neglected doing so; but there was more expression than truth of feeling in his letters, and the mail-day was not a pleasant epoch.

CHAPTER III.

TIME AND CHANGE.

WHILE Mr. Carteret lived, Robert Meredith had been a frequent visitor to Chayleigh. The quiet, eccentric old gentleman had remained in the old house, and had faithfully guarded his beloved collection to the last. But that emporium of curiosities had not received many additions after Mrs. Baldwin's death. The old man had taken, after a time, a little feeble pleasure in it, it is true; but only because those about him had acted on the hint which Margaret herself had given them, after the death of Mrs. Carteret, and persuaded him to resume his care of the collection because his daughter had been so fond of it.

Always quiet, uncomplaining, and kind to every one, the old man would have had rather a snubbed and subdued kind of life of it, under the rule of Haldane's bouncing Lucy, but for the vigilance of James Dugdale. That silent and unsuspected sufferer sedulously watched and cared for the old man, and Mrs. Haldane, who by no means liked him, so far respected and feared him that she never ventured to dispute any of his arrangements for Mr. Carteret's welfare.

He continued to like Lucy 'pretty well,' and to regard Robert Meredith with special favour, though he lived long enough to see Robert pass quite out of the category of exceptional boys. Indeed, so much did he like him, that at one time he entertained an idea of bequeathing to him the famous collection, after the demise of James Dugdale, who was to have a life interest in its delights and treasures ; but on the old gentle-

man's broaching the subject to him one
day, Robert Meredith put the objections to
the scheme so very strongly to him, that he
acknowledged the superior wisdom of his
young friend, bowed to his decision, and
liked him more than ever for his disinterestedness.

Robert represented to him that, though
the possession of the collection must afford
to any happy mortal capable of appreci-
ating it the purest and most lasting gratification, not so much the pleasure of the
individual as the preservation, the dignity,
and the safe keeping of the collection itself
ought to be considered. Unhappily, he,
Robert Meredith, was not likely to possess
a house in which the treasure might be
conveniently and suitably lodged, and it
was a melancholy fact that neither Haldane
nor his wife appreciated the collection; and,
when the present owner of Chayleigh should

be no more, and his bequest should have come into operation, there would arise the grievous necessity of dislodging the collection.

Under these circumstances—stated very carefully by Robert Meredith, who knew that his particular friend Mrs. Haldane would bundle both James and the collection out of doors with the smallest possible delay on the commencement of her absolute reign, unless indeed some very valuable consideration should attach itself to her not doing so—he suggested that Mr. Carteret would do well to conquer his objection to the 'merging' of the collection. That it should be 'merged' after his death was a less painful contingency to contemplate than that it should be destroyed or materially injured. The best, the most effectual plan would be, that Mr. Carteret should bequeath the collection, on James

Dugdale's death, to his granddaughter, the heiress of the Deane, with the request that it might be transferred thither, there to remain as an heirloom for ever. The old gentleman submitted with a sigh; and this testamentary arrangement was actually made.

The friendship between Robert and Mrs. Haldane, which had commenced in his boyish admiration of her, and her keen appreciation of the sentiment, remained unabated, which, considering that the pretty and vivacious Lucy was not conspicuous for steadiness of feeling, was not a little remarkable. Perhaps the lady believed in her secret soul, as the years wore on, that she could have explained Robert's not being a marrying man.

A strictly proper and virtuous British matron was Mrs. Haldane Carteret—a very dragon of propriety indeed, and a lady who would not have received her own

sister, if she had been so unlucky as to
'get talked of'—and therefore this insinua-
tion must be fully explained, in order to
prevent the slightest misapprehension on
the subject. Lucy would have been un-
speakably shocked had it ever been said or
thought by any one that Robert Meredith
entertained any feeling warmer than the
most strictly regulated friendship for her;
but she did not object to a secret sentiment
on her own part, which sometimes found
expression in reverie, and in a murmured
'poor boy,' in a little genial sense of satisfaction as the time went by and Robert did
not marry, and was not talked of as likely
to marry — when his polite attention to
her underwent no alteration, and she still
felt she enjoyed his confidence. Mrs. Haldane was a little mistaken in the latter
particular. She did *not* enjoy the confidence of Robert Meredith; but neither was

any other person in possession of that privilege, though it was one of the charms, or rather the achievements, of his manner, that he could convey the flattering impression to any one he pleased.

When Haldane and his wife were put, by the death of Mr. Carteret, in possession of Chayleigh — an event which occurred seven years after Margaret's decease, and four years later than that of Mr. Baldwin— James Dugdale continued to reside in the old house, which had been his home for so many years, only until the return of Lady Davyntry and her orphan nieces to England. Haldane Carteret, a 'good fellow' in all the popular acceptation of the word, was rather a weak fellow also, especially where his pretty wife's whims or feelings were concerned; and not all his sincere and grateful regard for his old friend could prevent his feeling relieved, when James

told him he could not resist Lady Davyntry's pressing entreaty that he should take
up his abode with her and 'the children.'
Every one spoke of the orphan girls as 'the
children,' and their fatherless and motherless estate was wonderfully tempered to
them.

The Deane had been let by Mr. Baldwin's executors for a long term of years;
but James Dugdale applied to the tenant
in possession for permission to have the
collection transferred thither, and received
it. Thus Mrs. Haldane was disembarrassed
within a very short period of her father-
in-law and his incomprehensible curiosities
and of James Dugdale. To do her justice,
Mrs. Haldane was sorry for the gentle,
quiet old man; and it certainly was not
with reference to him that she expressed
her satisfaction, when all the flittings had
been accomplished, in · 'being at last the

mistress of her own house.' There must have been a good deal of the imaginative faculty about Mrs. Haldane Carteret when she rejoiced in her freedom from trammels; for it never could have occurred to anybody that she had not been thoroughly and indisputably the mistress of Chayleigh from the day of her arrival there. But there is a great deal in imagination, and Mrs. Haldane knew her own business best.

When James Dugdale left Chayleigh, as a residence, for ever, the passion-flower which embowered the window of the room which had once been Margaret's, and had ever since been his, was in the full beauty and richness of its bloom. He cut a few twigs and leaves, and one or two of the grand solemn flowers, and took his leave of the room and the window and the tree. It was very painful, even after all those years—more painful than those to whom life is full of activity and change could conceive or would believe. But so thoroughly was this a final parting, and so truly did James Dugdale feel it so, that when, some time afterwards, Mrs. Haldane, having read in some new medical treatise that 'green things'—as she generally termed everything that grew, from the cedar of Lebanon to the parsley of private life— were unwholesome on the walls of a house, had the passion-flower and the trellis cleared away, and the wall above the verandah neatly whitewashed, it hardly gave him a pang.

In all the changes which befell the family at Chayleigh, Robert Meredith had a certain share. Mr. Carteret never ceased to like him, to look for his coming, to enjoy, in his quiet way, the adaptive young man's society. James never permitted the interest he had taken in him for his old friend's sake—his old friend dead and gone now, like all the rest—to flag or falter. Perhaps he held by that feeling all the more conscientiously that he had never been much drawn towards Robert Meredith individually. The feeling towards him which he and Margaret had shared at the first had remained with him always, like all his feelings; for it was part of the constitution of his mind, a part powerful for suffering, that he did not change.

When Lady Davyntry went abroad with 'the children' James Dugdale's life had become more than ever solitary; and, though conscious that he derived very little pleasure from Robert's presence, he encouraged the visits which Mrs. Haldane was ever ready to invite.

But a day of still greater change came —a sad and heavy day to James Dugdale, and of tremendous loss and evil to the orphan girls. Lady Davyntry died—not suddenly, but unexpectedly—and the full responsibility of the guardianship of Gertrude and Eleanor Baldwin was thrown upon Haldane Carteret and James Dugdale. Davyntry, in which Mr. Baldwin's sister had only a life interest, passed into the possession of the young man who had succeeded to the title on the death of Sir Richard Davyntry; and the choice of the guardians to the young girls, as to the future home of their wards, lay between Chayleigh and the Deane, of which it became possible for them to resume possession shortly after Lady Davyntry's death.

When the decision which assigned the Deane to the young heiresses as their future abode had been reached and acted upon, Robert Meredith naturally ceased to have much intercourse with the Carterets and with James Dugdale.

Haldane was very much pleased with the kind of life he led at the Deane. He made a first-rate 'country gentleman,' an ardent sportsman, a pleasant companion, hospitable, kind-hearted, *insouciant*, fond of the place and of everything in it, devoted to his wife—'absurdly so,' as the spinsters of the neighbourhood, a remarkably numerous class even for Scotland, declared—and most indulgent and affectionate to his nieces. This latter quality the aforesaid spinsters accounted for satisfactorily on the double grounds, that it was not likely he would be anything but indulgent to such rich girls—of course he expected to be well recompensed when they came into 'all their property'—and that, as he had no children of his own, he might very well care for his 'poor dear sister's fatherless girls.'

The worthy ex-captain of artillery knew little and cared less how people accounted

for the strange phenomena of his fulfilling
carefully and conscientiously a sacred duty.
He was a good, happy, unsuspicious man,
and 'the children' loved him better than
any one in the world, except James Dugdale and Rose Doran.

Mrs. Carteret was in the habit of 'going
south' much more frequently than Haldane
did so; she liked a few weeks in London
in the season, and she scrupulously visited
her own family, by whom she was regarded
with much affection and admiration, not
quite unmingled with awe.

The eldest Miss Crofton's 'match' had
'turned out' much better than the family
had expected, and Lucy Carteret shone
very brilliantly indeed in the reflected light
shed upon her by the wealth and station
of her husband's nieces and wards. On
the occasion of her visits to England she
always saw a good deal of Robert Mere-

dith; and so—owing to the convenience of
modern locomotion, Mrs. Carteret's former
home had been brought within easy reach
of London—Robert was a not unfrequent
guest of old Mr. Crofton's when his daughter was sojourning there. Chayleigh had
been advantageously let by Haldane for
some years beyond the term of his nieces'
minority.

On the last occasion of her 'going south'
Mrs. Carteret had been accompanied by
Eleanor Baldwin, whose health, always delicate, had recently occasioned her uncle
and aunt some anxiety. She had enjoyed
her trip, and Robert had been very much
with both ladies. Never had Mrs. Carteret been more thoroughly convinced
that he was one of the most charming of men; never had the secret suspicion, that she could, if she chose, explain the reason of his having remained

up to his present age unmarried, presented itself so frequently and so strongly to her mind.

Robert Meredith had been told by Mrs. Carteret that Haldane intended to celebrate the attainment of her majority by the heiress of the Deane in splendid style, and he had received from her a pressing invitation to be present on the occasion. The time of year made it difficult for him to feel sure of being able to leave town; but he promised that he would go to the Deane on that auspicious and delightful occasion, then six months in perspective, if he could possibly manage it.

It was during this visit of Mrs. Carteret to London that George Ritherdon made her acquaintance, and saw for the first time one of 'the Baldwin children,' of whom he had heard occasional casual mention. Robert Meredith's 'chum' pleased Mrs. Carteret much, especially when he did the honours of the Temple Church to her and Eleanor; and while explaining all the objects of interest and their associations, did so with a happy and successful assumption of merely refreshing their memory, which was indicative of the nicest tact. The general result was that, when Robert Meredith received a formal reminder of his promise to come to the Deane for Gertrude's birthday, the letter enclosed a pressing invitation to George Ritherdon to accompany his friend.

'Of course you'll come. There's much less to keep you in town than there is to keep me, for that matter, so you can't pretend to object,' said Meredith, as the friends were discussing their letters and their breakfast simultaneously.

'I should like it very much indeed,' said Ritherdon; 'but—'

'Very well, of course you'll do it,' interrupted Meredith; and was about to say something more, when the entrance of their 'mutual' servant suspended the conversation.

The man addressed himself to Robert, with the information that a person was then waiting in the passage, who urgently requested to be admitted to see him; that the person was an old man, not of remarkably prosperous appearance; and that he had replied to the servant's remonstrance, on his presenting himself at such an unseemly hour, that he was sure Mr. Meredith would see him, for he came from Australia, and from his own 'people' there.

Surprised, but by no means discomposed, Robert Meredith made no reply to the servant, but said to George Ritherdon,

'It sounds odd. I suppose I ought to see him.'

'I think so, old fellow; and I'll clear off;' which he did.

'Show the old person from Australia in, William,' said Meredith to the servant, and added to himself, 'I wonder what he has got to say to me—nothing I need mind. I should have had bad news by post, if there was any to send.'

CHAPTER IV.

THE HEIRESS OF THE DEANE.

'Are you nearly ready, girls?' asked Mrs. Haldane Carteret of her nieces, as she entered the large dressing-room which divided the bedrooms occupied by Gertrude and Eleanor Baldwin, and was joint territory, common to them both.

This apartment was very handsomely proportioned, and furnished in a sumptuous style. It abounded in light and looking-glasses, and the two young girls then under the hands of their respective maids had the advantage of seeing themselves reflected many times in mirrors fixed and mirrors movable. Their ball-room toilette was almost complete, and the smaller sup-

plementary articles of their paraphernalia
of adornment were strewn about the room
in pretty profusion.

'We are very nearly ready, aunt Lucy,'
replied Eleanor; 'are there any people
come yet?'

'Yes, the Congreves, and Rennies, and
Comrie of Largs; they always make a
point of being the first arrivals and the
last departures everywhere,' said Mrs. Carteret, as she profited by the long mirror
which formed the reverse of the door by
which she had entered to rearrange the folds
of her remarkably becoming dress of blue
satin and silver. 'Pray make haste, Gerty.
It does not so much matter about Nelly,
but you really must be in the reception-
room before any more people come. Just
imagine your not being there when Lord
and Lady Gelston arrive, or even Sir Mait-
land and Lady Cardeness.'

Mrs. Haldane Carteret was a woman of perfectly well - proportioned mind. She knew how to define the distinctions of rank as accurately as a king-at-arms, and could balance the comparative turpitude of a slight to a baron with that of a slight to a baronet with quite a mathematical nicety of precision.

'Almost ready, aunt Lucy. Only my gloves and bracelets to put on, and then I am ready. But I certainly shall not go down without Nelly; she would get on much better without me than I should without her' (here the girl smiled as her mother had smiled in the brief days of her happy and contented love). 'We should have been ready sooner, but that we took a final scamper off to the guests' rooms to see how Rose had disposed of Mr. Meredith and Mr. Ritherdon.'

'Ah, by the bye, I suppose they have

arrived,' said Mrs. Carteret; 'I must go
and see them. I will come back again, and
I hope you will both be ready.'

In a few minutes the preparations were
complete, and the two young girls were
receiving the unequivocal compliments of
their maids and their mirrors. Happy,
joyous, hopeful, handsome creatures they
looked, as they stood, their arms entwined,
surveying their lithe, graceful, white-robed
figures with natural pride and very par-
donable vanity. The glance of the elder
girl dwelt only passingly upon herself; it
turned then to dwell upon her sister with
delight, with exultation.

'How beautiful you look, my darling
Nelly! I am sure no one in the room will
be able to compare with you to-night.'

'Not you, Gertrude? Are you not the
queen of the ball in every sense? Depend upon it, no one will have eyes to-

night for any one except the heiress of the Deane.'

' Then every one will be blind and foolish,' returned Gertrude, as she gave the speaker a sisterly push; 'and there are a few whom I don't think that of, Nelly. Don't you dread the idea of the speech-making at supper ? I do, and uncle Haldane does, because he will have to return thanks for me ; and I'm sure everybody else does, because Lord Gelston is so frightfully long-winded and historical, and so tremendously well up in the history of all the Meritons and all the Baldwins, and who married, and whom, and when they did it, and there's no stopping him when he starts ; however, we must think of the dancing and the fun, and not remember the dreadful speeches until they come to be made.'

' I daresay you won't mind them so much when the time comes,' said Nelly, with the least touch of something unpleasant in her voice; 'at all events, I need not — they will not make any speeches about *me*, that's a comfort!'

'My darling Nelly! as if I thought about it for *myself*. If you must listen and look pleased at tiresomeness, what does it matter of what is *apropos?* and where is the difference between you and me?'

'Very present, very perceptible, after this day,' said Nelly; 'no one will fail to keep it in mind. Did you not notice what aunt Lucy said? My being ready or not did not matter, but the presence of "the heiress of the Deane" was indispensable.'

'I did hear it,' said Gertrude, turning a flushed cheek and a deprecatory glance upon her sister; 'and did you not hear what I said? But here come aunt Lucy and Rose.'

The entry of Rose Doran was the sig-

nal for enthusiastic comments on the appearance of the two young girls, and the
little cloud which had threatened for a
moment to gather over the sisters was
joyously dissipated. Mr. Dugdale wished
to see them in his sitting-room, Rose said,
before they went downstairs, and she had
come to bring them to him.

'You'll have time enough to let the
old gentleman have a peep at you, my
darlings,' said the good woman, whose
eyes were moist with the rising tears pro-
duced by many associations which almost
overpowered the admiration and delight
with which she regarded the girls; 'though
there's a dale o' quality come, they're all
in the study, makin' sure of their cloaks
and things, or drinkin' coffee and chattin'
to one another. So go to the old man, my
girls; he won't keep ye a minute.'

'He surely won't disappoint us,' exclaimed Gertrude; 'he promised to come down, and he *must!*'

'So he will, alanna,' said Rose, using the same term of endearment, and in the same soothing tone, with which she had been wont to assuage Gertrude's griefs in her childhood—'never you fear, so he will, when the room is full, and he can get round behind the people to his own chair in the corner; only he wants a look at you all to himself first.'

'Then I will go on,' said Mrs. Haldane in rather a vexed tone. 'You will find me in the morning room; and pray, Gerty, make no delay.'

Then Mrs. Haldane walked majestically away, her blue and silver train rustling superbly over the crimson-velvet carpet of the long, wide corridor, which, like the grand staircase, was of polished oak.

Mr. Dugdale's rooms at the Deane were

in a quiet and secluded part of the spacious house, attainable by a small staircase which was approached by a curtained archway opening off the corridor into which the girls' rooms opened. The rooms were handsome, though not large, and were luxuriously furnished, but they were chiefly remarkable for the numerous evidences of feminine care, taste, and industry in their arrangement. The comfortable and the ornamental were dexterously united in these rooms, in which needlework abounded, and whose most prized decorations were the work of the pencils of the two girls.

The apartments consisted of three rooms — bedroom, dressing-room, and sitting-room, the latter lined with books, and bearing many indications that the studies, tastes, and habits which had occupied James Dugdale's youth and manhood had lightened the burden of his infirmities, and taken the deadly sting out of his sorrows, were not abandoned now in his old age. And in truth this was the case; the feebleness which had invaded the delicate and sensitive frame more and more surely with each succeeding year, had not touched the mind. That was strong, active, bright, full of vitality still, promising extinction or even dimness only with the dissolution of the frame.

In his frequent fits of thinking about himself, and yet out of himself—as though he were contemplating the problems presented by the existence, and pondering the future, of another — James Dugdale was wont to wonder at his own tenacity of life. Ever since his youth he had been a sufferer in body, and had sustained great trials of mind; he had been always more or less feeble, and of the nervous febrile temperament which is said (erroneously) to wear itself out rapidly. But he had lived on and on, and the young, the strong, the prosperous, the happy, had passed before him, and been lost in the dimness of the separation of death.

He had been carefully dressed by his servant for the festivities of the evening, and had laid down upon the couch beside the windows of his sitting-room, from which a beautiful view was to be had in the day-time, through which the summer moonlight was streaming now, and had fallen into a reverie. His mind was singularly placid, his memory was singularly clear to-night, as he lay still, listening to the stir in the house, his face turned from the light of the candles which burned on the tables and the mantelpiece; and passing in mental review the persons and the events of long years ago.

How perfectly distinct and vivid they were to-night—his parents, his boyhood, the time when it was first discovered that he must never expect to be a healthy, vigorous man—his student days and their associations, the friends of that period of his life! Hayes Meredith was a young man —how curiously his memory reproduced him; and then his cousin Sibylla, his sole kinswoman and his steady friend—the old man who had loved him so well, and the sad dark episode of Margaret's marriage. How plainly he could see Godfrey Hunger-ford, and how distinctly he could recall the instinctive dislike, suspicion, repulsion he had caused him, and which he early learnt to know was bitter jealousy! Baldwin and Lady Davyntry, that kind, sympathising friend of later days—she whom he still mourned with a poignancy which time had blunted in the case of the others;—it was hard to understand, very wonderful to realise, that they were dead and he alive— he went on with his ordinary life betimes, and did not think about it much, but to-night it seemed impossible.

The wonderful incompleteness, the un-meaningness of life, the phantasmagoria of fragmentary existences occupied him, while all around him were preparations for a festival. Lastly came the image of Mar-garet, back in all the freshness of her youth, beauty, and happiness, as she had been twenty years ago, and the old man wondered at the strange distinctness of his memory.

Twenty years! a long, long time even at an earlier period of life, a wonder-fully long time at his, to keep the memory green. He had had and lost many friends, but only one love; yes, that was the ex-planation; that was why she, who had died

young long ago, never to grow old, never
to have any withering touch of time laid
upon her beauty, she who was to be remembered as a radiant creature always,
had never had a predecessor, a successor,
or a rival in his heart; so there was no
other image to trouble or confuse hers.
The circumstances which had killed her, as
he felt, as surely as disease had ever killed,
—they, too, returned freshly to his memory;
he seemed to live through those old, old
days again, and in some degree to realise
once more their keen anxiety and distress.

How it had all passed away—how little
it had really mattered—how little anything
really mattered, after all, except the other
world, and the reunion there, without which
life, the most renowned as much as the
meanest, would indeed be 'a tale told by an
idiot,' and, in the multitude of the ages, and
the spanlike brevity of its own duration,

'signifying nothing'! It seemed like a dream, and yet it was all real : she had lived and suffered, feared, foreseen, and died under this very roof, beneath which he dwelt, and from which its master went forth a patient, but none the less a broken-hearted man, to die afar off, to lie in the solemn dust of the grand old world.

Were they, the two whom he remembered so well in their youth and love and happiness, any nearer to him than the most ancient of the ancient dead? Was there any difference or degree in all that inconceivable separation? Who could tell him that? Who could still the pang, which time can never lessen, which comes with the immeasurable change? We are in time and space, and they, the dead, are, as we say, beyond their bounds, set free from them. What, then, is their share with us?

He was thinking of these things, which indeed were wont to occupy his mind when he was very peaceful and alone, and thinking also how very brief all our uncertainty is—how short a time the Creator keeps His creatures in ignorance and suspense, and that he was very near to the lifting of the curtain—when Gertrude and Eleanor Baldwin came into the room, and gaily challenged his admiration of their ball-dresses, their wreaths, their bouquets, and their general appearance.

With the keenly strong remembrance of Margaret which he had been dwelling upon freshly before him, James Dugdale was struck by the likeness which Gertrude presented to her mother. Her face was more strictly handsome, her figure promised to be fuller and grander, but the resemblance in feature, in gesture, in voice, in all the subtler affinities which constitute the truth

of such resemblances, was complete. Had
she stood thus, in her white dress, flower
crowned, by his couch, alone, James Dugdale might have thought the spirit world
had unbarred its portals for a little to give
him a glimpse of Margaret in her eternal
youth; but her arm was linked in that of
her sister, and the old man's gaze included
them both.

'Do I like you, you witches?' said Mr.
Dugdale; 'what a question! I think you
are both incomparably perfect, and among
all the compliments you will hear to-night,
I don't think you will have a more satisfactory one than that. I see you are wearing your pearls, Nelly.—Where are your
diamonds, Miss Baldwin?'

Gertrude blushed, and looked a little
uncomfortable.

'I would rather not wear them,' she
said; 'pearls don't matter much, but dia-

monds would make too much difference between Nelly and me. I asked uncle Haldane, and he said I certainly need not wear them unless I liked; indeed, he said it is better taste for an unmarried woman, while she is very young, not to wear diamonds; so they are undisturbed in all their grandeur.'

'Isn't she ridiculous?' said Eleanor. 'I am sure if I were in her place I should wear my diamonds, especially to-night.'

'I am quite sure you would do no such thing, Nelly,' said Miss Baldwin; 'and we must go now, or aunt Lucy will be put out.—Mind you come down soon; I shall be looking out for you.'

Then the two girls kissed the old man affectionately and left him. There was some trouble in James Dugdale's mind when the light forms disappeared, and he listened to the murmur of their voices for a few moments, before it died away when they reached the grand staircase.

'If Eleanor were in Gertrude's place!' The girl's words had struck a chord of painful remembrance in the old man's mind. The time had come now when the wrong done to the younger by the elder, the wrong done to the children by the parents in all unconsciousness, was to bear its first fruits. As the years had gone by, and especially since Lady Davyntry's death had left James Dugdale sole possessor of the knowledge of the truth, he had remembered it but seldom.

When the news of Mr. Baldwin's death had reached England, he and Lady Davyntry had spoken together much and solemnly of the mysterious dealings of Providence with the family. They had silently accepted his resolution—never to give Margaret a successor in his heart and house—

and, in view of that determination, they had regarded the arrangement which he had made of his property as in every respect wise and commendable. But they had secretly hoped that time, whose unfailing influence, however disliked or even struggled against, they both had too much experience of life to doubt or dispute, would modify and finally upset Mr. Baldwin's resolution on that point, and that the girls might eventually be removed from what they wisely regarded as a perilous and undesirable position. Wealth and station would always be theirs, even if a second marriage should give a male heir to the Deane.

But these hopes were not destined to be realised. Mr. Baldwin never returned from his journey to the East, and the heavy weight of heiress-ship fell upon his daughters in their childhood. Of late years the secret of which he alone was in possession had begun to appear dreamlike and mythical to James Dugdale. It had been a terrible thing in its time, but that time was past and its terror with it, and it was only an old memory now—an old memory which Nelly's words had awakened, just when he did not care to have it evoked, just when it was as painful as it ever could be any more.

The old man rose from his couch and went to a bookcase with glass doors, which faced the mantelpiece in his sitting-room. On one of the lower shelves, within easy reach of his hand, lay a large blue-velvet casket. He took it out, set it on the table, and opened it. It contained a picture—the portrait of Margaret with her infant in her arms, which she had had painted for him at Naples twenty years before. The portrait was surrounded by a frame of peculiar design. It consisted of a wreath of passion-flowers, the stems and leaves in gold, the flowers in white enamel, with every detail of form and colouring accurately carried out. This was the only jeweller's work which had ever been done by James Dugdale's order; this was the most valuable article in every sense in his possession. He placed the picture on the table, and sat down before it and looked at it intently, studying in every line the likeness which had impressed him so deeply to-night; and then he replaced it in the casket, which he reconsigned to the bookcase. This done, he rang for his servant and went down to the ball-room, whence delightful strains of brilliant music were issuing, blended with the sound of voices and the tread of dancing feet.

The scene was a beautiful one. All that money, taste, and goodwill could accomplish to render the fête given in cele-

bration of Gertrude's birthday successfully
charming, had been done, and the result
was eminently satisfactory. Many of the
guests had come from distances which in
England would have been regarded as invincible obstacles—would indeed have rendered the sending of invitations a meaningless, or according to our amiable insular
phrase a ' French,' compliment—but which
in Scotland were regarded as mere matters of course. An unusual number of
pretty girls adorned the ball-room, and
they danced with pleasure and animation
also peculiarly Scotch.

Gertrude had gone through the ordeal
of congratulation very well; and now, very
much relieved that that part of the business had come to a conclusion, was dancing
a surprisingly animated quadrille with Lord
Gelston, while Lady Gelston was talking
superlatives to Haldane Carteret, who had

wisely decided, some years before, on coming to live in Scotland, that there was more
to be gained than lost by being understood
at once to be excluded from the category
of dancing men.

The room, much longer than its width,
and beautifully decorated and lighted, was
amply occupied without being overfilled;
and the splendid many-coloured dresses,
the moving figures, the soft sound of
speech and laughter, the indescribable joyous rustle which pervades an assemblage
where youth and beauty are in the majority, made up a scene to whose attraction
James Dugdale's nerves vibrated strangely.
He had been present on few similar occasions in his life, and he looked about him
with the pleased curiosity of a child. The
military contingent had duly arrived from
Edinburgh, Leith, and Hamilton, and were
enjoying their accustomed popularity.

Of the many faces in the room there were few known to James Dugdale, with the exception of those of the near neighbours to the Deane. Before he had time to become familiar with the movement and the glitter of the unaccustomed scene, a pause occurred in the dancing, and the group nearest to him broke up and moved away. Then he saw Eleanor Baldwin talking to a gentleman whose figure seemed very familiar to him, though he could not see his face. Eleanor was looking up at the gentleman, her face full of light and animation, a rich colour in her cheeks, her dark eyes sparkling with pleasure. Almost as soon as he saw her, she saw him, and said :

' O, there's uncle James, let us go and speak to him.'

She walked quickly across the room, followed by her companion, who was, as

James Dugdale then perceived, Robert Meredith. The old man and the man no longer young indeed, but still and ever a boy to him, greeted each other warmly.

'When did you come, Robert? Why have I not seen you before?'

'We came down by the mail, sir, and found the ladies gone to dress; and Mrs. Doran said you were resting, in preparation for the fatigue of the evening, so we would not disturb you. I am glad to see you looking so well, sir.'

'Thank you, Robert—where's Ritherdon?'

'He has gone in chase of Gerty, uncle James,' said Eleanor; 'he wants to know what dances she can spare him, I believe; but I fancy he has not much chance— even *I* could only promise positively for one.'

Robert Meredith looked at her narrowly as he said :

'Ritherdon has pluck, I must say. I never dreamed of such a privilege as dancing to-night with the lady of the Deane. But I did calculate upon a *raccroc de noces* for to-morrow—I suppose that's safe ?'

'I suppose so,' said Eleanor.

'*You* kept a few dances for me, didn't you ?' he asked.

'Yes, I did, but I am nobody, you know.'

'This is one of them,' said Meredith, and then, as he led her away into the throng, again set in motion by the music, he said meaningly, 'and I do not know,— at least, *I do.*'

His arm was round her now, and he had whirled her into the circle of waltzers, and the girl felt that the bright scene was brighter, the music sweeter and more in-

spiriting, the dance more delightful, because of the words and the tone in which
he had spoken them.

George Ritherdon had been quite as
unsuccessful in his quest as Eleanor had
foreseen, and as soon as Gertrude had convinced him of his ill-fortune, by permitting
him to read the record of the pretty little
ivory and silver *carnet* which hung at her
waist, he, in his turn, made his way to
Mr. Dugdale's chair. There he remained
until Nelly's one dance should be 'due,'
talking with the old man, who was wonderfully bright and unwearied of things in
general, and of the young ladies in particu-
cular.

It was an unfashionable peculiarity of
George Ritherdon's that he was always
deferential towards age, even when age
was much less venerable and less intelli-
gent, much more *arrière* than in the case

of Mr. Dugdale. Therefore, let the sub-
jects on which the old gentleman had
chosen to talk with him have been as dull
and uninteresting to him as possible, he
would have exerted himself to converse
about them pleasantly, and with the air of
attention and interest which is the truest
conversational politeness.

But in the present instance no effort
was required. Ritherdon felt a sincere and
growing interest in the ' children,' as Mr.
Dugdale soon began to call them in talking
to him, and found something which appealed to his heart—strangely soft, pure,
and upright in its impulses, considering the
length of time it had pulsated amid the
world,—in the long-enduring, constant family friendship which bound the old man's
life up with that of these young people,
who were no kin of his. The ball was the
gayest, the most successful, in George Ri-

therdon's opinion, at which he had ever 'assisted,' the night a happy and memorable one in his life; but no part of it was more thoroughly enjoyable to him than the time he passed seated by the old man's side, their conversation interrupted only by the people who came up to speak to Mr. Dugdale, and by the girls, who paid him flying visits.

Robert Meredith and his friend saw little of each other during the night, until after James Dugdale had retired, which he did when supper was announced. That sumptuous entertainment was as terrible an ordeal as Gertrude had expected. Lord Gelston was as inexorably long-winded, as overwhelmingly genealogical as usual; and if anything could have made her more uncomfortable than the ponderous congratulations of the noble lord, and the marked attentions of Lady Gelston and the Honour-

able Mr. Dort, the eldest son of the distinguished but by no means wealthy pair,
it would have been the kindly but inart-
istic efforts of her uncle Haldane, who was
neither a ready thinker nor an adept at
speaking, to express how far short of her
personal qualities fell the gifts of wealth
and station allotted to her.

A very decent amount of general attention was bestowed upon Lord Gelston and
Haldane Carteret, and the speeches of both
were received with all proper enthusiasm;
but there was one listener who heard them
with more than the attention of politeness,
and with a smile on his lips which, if ' the
children's' dead mother saw it, must have
reminded ·her of one she had known and
disliked in earthly days long ago. But
even the speeches were over at last, and
the younger guests left the banquet and
returned to the ball-room, and dancing re-

commenced. Nothing equals in vigour and
perseverance Scotch dancing, no entertainment is capable of such preternatural pro-
longation as a Scotch ball. The institution
might be the modern successor of the feasts
of the Norsemen in the Bersekyr days.

'Do these people ever intend to leave
off, do you think?' George Ritherdon asked
of Robert Meredith, when the external light
had become difficult of exclusion, and all
the dowagers had given over talking and
taking refreshment, except that of slum-
ber.

'I don't know indeed ; doesn't look like
it ; but there's no reason why we shouldn't,'
returned Meredith ; 'let us say good-morn-
ing to Mrs. Carteret, and decamp.'

A masterly manœuvre, which they put
into instant execution, unobserved by any
one but Eleanor Baldwin. She had danced
several times with Meredith during the

night, and had contrived to give Ritherdon 'one more' in addition to the promised valse; she had been very gay, happy, and animated; much admired and fully conscious of it; but now she grew tired, and began to wish the ball were over. People were unreasonable to keep it up so late; this was making a toil of a pleasure; no, she really could not join in this interminable cotillon. She wondered whether aunt Lucy would mind her leaving the room; she would find her and ask her. So she did find Mrs. Haldane Carteret, who was looking rather yellow and elderly in the mixed intrusive light, and Mrs. Haldane answered her rather snappishly,

'Yes, yes, of course you may go. It is really absurdly late; no wonder you're tired; I am sure I am. Gerty must remain of course, but you may go.'

Eleanor had got the permission she desired, and she left the room, but not gladly. The manner of that permission did not please her; many little things of the same kind had hurt her lately; and as she slowly mounted the stairs her face was dark, and she muttered to herself,

'Gerty must of course remain, but you may go.'

An hour later, when the morning had fairly asserted its sway, when the latest lingering of the guests not staying in the house had departed, fortified by hot strong coffee against the fatigue of their home-ward route, when to those staying in the house welcome announcement had been made that breakfast was to be served at twelve, and continued for an indefinite time,—Gertrude Baldwin entered her dress-ing-room. She had desired that her maid should not remain up, and having glanced into Eleanor's bedroom and seen that she was asleep, she took off her ball-dress, set the windows wide open, and sat down in her dressing-gown, letting the sweet morning air play upon her face to calm the hurry of her spirits and to think.

This had been an eventful day for that young girl ; indeed, the whole preceding week, during which her guardians, Haldane Carteret and James Dugdale, had explained to her in resigning their trust all the particulars of her position, had been of great moment in her life. Previously she had known, vaguely, that she was very rich, and she had had a tolerably clear notion of the origin and ordering of her wealth, but she fully understood it now. Her uncle had wished her to give her attention to the accounts of the estate, as he explained them to her, and she had complied with his wish. In the course of these transactions, she had been shown her father's will, and had been made acquainted as minutely with her sister Eleanor's position as with her own.

The time up to that day had been so full of business, and all the hours of the day and night just gone had been so full of pleasure, that she felt strongly the need of a little leisure and solitude now. She was glad Nelly was asleep, glad she had not been obliged to talk over the ball with her —glad to put the ball itself out of her thoughts for a little, although she had enjoyed it with all the unaffected zest of her age.

Gertrude was not tired; she had danced incessantly, and the emotions of the day had been many and various; but she was strong and very happy, in all the unruffled peace of her girlhood, which had only progressed hitherto in prosperity, and she rarely felt fatigue. The fresh morning air, the calm, the solitude, were better for her than sleep. Presently a delicious stillness fell on everything; no more doors were shut or opened, no desultory footsteps loitered about; the birds' music only filled the air with the most beautiful of the sounds of morning.

There came with the day to Gertrude a sense of change. She realised her woman-hood now—she realised her position, and it appeared to her a very solemn and respon-sible one. Her uncle had told her, in ans-wer to her request, that he would continue to exercise the functions from which the attainment of her majority formally dis-charged him—that he would do so provided she would take an active part in the con-duct of the estate, urging the necessity which existed for her duly qualifying her-self for the independent administration of her affairs in the future. He reminded her that she could only hold the property in trust for her children, if she were destined to become a wife and mother, and must therefore learn how to save from her large income.

'You see, my dear,' Haldane had said to her, 'everything not included in the entail is left absolutely to Nelly, and in this respect she is better off than you are. She is not indeed so rich, but she can dispose of her property, by settlement and by will, just as she pleases, whereas you cannot dispose of a shilling. Your eldest son, or your eldest daughter, if you have no son, must inherit all. The estate is chargeable for the benefit of younger children to a very small extent. I will show you how and how much presently. The fortune your grandfather gave to to your aunt, Lady Davyntry, and which Eleanor inherits from her, was almost en-

tirely derived from accumulations and other
extraneous property. So, you see, Nelly's
money is more absolutely hers than yours
is yours; but though you have not so much
freedom, there is one advantage in your
position. If you fall into bad hands, which
God forbid, and we will take all possible
care to prevent—yes, Gerty, don't look so
horrified, my child, all the men in the world
are not good, as your poor mother could
have told you—your money will be safe;
no man can beggar *you;* whereas Eleanor
would be quite helpless in such a case.
There is nothing to protect her ; her husband, if he could only persuade her to
marry without a strict settlement, could
make ducks and drakes of her money, if he
chose.'

'But surely she never would be persuaded to do anything so foolish and so
unprincipled,' said Gertrude, with a pretty

air of dignity, woman-of-the-worldishness, and landed proprietor combined, and feeling already as if she had the deepest appreciation of the rights, privileges, and duties of property.

'I don't know that, my dear,' said Haldane; 'women are easily persuaded to folly, and there are men who have a knack of persuading you that imprudence is generosity, and self-sacrifice proved by endangering other people's peace and prosperity—as your poor mother could also have told you. However, we need not make ourselves prematurely uncomfortable about Nelly. Let us hope her choice may be wise and happy, and that she may use the freedom her father and her aunt left her with discretion.'

The discussion then turned upon other matters of business, and this part of the subject was abandoned.

It returned to Gertrude Baldwin's thoughts as she looked pensively abroad on her wide domains in the early morning, and it troubled her.

'We were both so little when he left us,' she thought, 'that I don't think my father could have preferred Nelly very much to me, and my mother only saw her for a minute before she died. Rose told me she had scarcely strength to hold the baby to her breast, and not strength enough to speak a word to it, so she cannot have loved her more than me; I was with her for a little time—it is very strange. What care has been taken to give her all he could give; and nothing left to me for my own self, on account of my own self! And how strange uncle James looked when I said so! I am sure he understands that I feel it and wonder at it.

'How little I know of my mother, and

I so like her, he says! Perhaps I am old enough now for them to tell me more about her and that first marriage of hers, which I am sure must have been something dreadful. I will ask uncle James some day when he is very well. Aunt Lucy has never told us anything but that she and mamma were great friends, and mamma was "a dear thing. Somehow I don't like to hear our dear dead mother spoken of as "a dear thing"—absurd, I daresay, but I do not; and dear aunt Eleanor never talked of her as anything but papa's wife—his idolised wife.

'How well I remember when I first began to understand that he died of her loss in reality, though it took time to kill him, because he was good and patient and tried to be resigned! But he could not live longer without her, and God knew it and did not ask him. I remember so well when aunt Eleanor told me that, and seemed to know it so well, that she could better bear to know that he was dead than to know that he was still wandering about, because there was no home for him here. I wonder was he very fond of us—or perhaps he was not able to be. I am sure he tried. Ah, well! this we can never, never know until we are orphan children no longer; and any doubt dishonours him.

'To think that I am so important a personage, the owner of a great estate, the employer of so many of my fellow-creatures, —with so much power in my weak woman's hands for good or for evil,—and that I am all this solely because of great misfortune —solely because I am an orphan! If they were living, there might indeed have been rejoicing here to-day, for our pleasure and our parents' pride; but no more. It is wonderful to think of that,—wonderful to

think of what might have been. Shall I
be a good woman, I wonder? Shall I be a
faithful steward? I don't know—I am so
ignorant; but for uncle James, I am so
lonely. At least I will try—for my father's
sake, and mamma's, and his, and for my
own sake and for God's; but O, I wish, I
wish I could have found in my father's
will anything, however trifling, which he
desired to come to me from him, for my
own sake.'

Tears were standing in the dark, clear
gray eyes of the young lady of the Deane,
and she had forgotten all about the birthday ball.

CHAPTER V.

THE breakfast-table at the Deane was but scantily furnished with guests at noon on the day after the ball, and only among the younger portion of that restricted number did the spirit of 'talking it over' prevail. The gentlemen, with the exception of George Ritherdon, discussed their breakfast and their newspapers, and the matrons were decidedly sleepy and a little cross. George was in high spirits. He had very thorough notions on the subject of enjoying a holiday, and he included among them the delight of escaping from the obligation of reading newspapers.

' Look at your friend, Mr. What's-his-
name, of some queer place, like Sir Walter
Scott's novels,' he whispered to Gertrude.
' The idea of coming on a brief visit to
Paradise, and troubling your head about
foreign politics and the money - market!
There he goes—Prussia, indeed! What a
combination of ideas—Bochum Dollfs and
the Deane !'

Gertrude laughed. The pleasant unaffected gaiety of his manner pleased her.
She had not been prepared to find George
Ritherdon so light of heart, so ready to be
amused, and to acknowledge it. She knew
that he was younger than his chum Robert
Meredith; but she had fancied there would
be some resemblance between them, when
she should come to know them better, in
a few days' close association with them.
But there was no resemblance; the friendship between them, the daily companion-

ship had brought about no assimilation,
and there was one circumstance which set
Gerty thinking and puzzling to find out
why it should be so. She had known
Robert Meredith for years; her acquaintance with George Ritherdon was of the
slightest; and yet, when the day after the
ball came in its turn to a conclusion, and
she once again set her mind to the task of
'thinking it over,' she felt that she knew
more of George Ritherdon, had seen more
certain indications of his disposition, and
could divine more of his life than she knew,
had seen, or could divine in the case of
Robert Meredith. The girl was of a
thoughtful speculative turn of mind, an
observer of character, and imaginative. She
pondered a good deal upon the subject, and
constantly recurred to her first thought.
' How odd it is that I should feel as if
I could tell at once how Mr. Ritherdon

would act in any given case, and I don't
feel that in the least about Robert Meredith!'

'I was horribly ill-treated last night,'
George said, after he and Gertrude had
exchanged ideas on the subject of newspapers in vacation time. 'You ask me to
a ball, Miss Baldwin, and then don't give
me a dance. I call it treacherous and in-
hospitable.'

'I couldn't help it,' said Gerty earn-
estly, with perfect simplicity. 'I had to
" dance down the set," as they say in the
country dances—to begin at the beginning
of the table of precedence, and go on to
the end.'

'A very unfair advantage for the
fogeys,' said George Ritherdon, not without having made sure that none of Gertrude's partners of last night were at the
table.

'The Honourable Dort would be grateful if he heard you, Ritherdon,' observed Meredith.

'I suppose one couldn't reasonably call *him* a fogey,' returned George.

Gertrude laughed; but Eleanor said sharply,

'No, he is only a fool.'

Meredith was seated next her, and while the others went on talking, he said to her in a low tone,

'Do you think him a fool? I don't. He knows the value of first impressions, and being early in the field, or I am much mistaken.'

If Robert Meredith had made a similar remark to Gertrude, she would simply have looked at him with her grave gray eyes, in utter ignorance of his meaning; but Nelly understood him perfectly.

'He *is* an admirer of Gerty's,' she said.

'And a more ardent admirer of the Deane,' said Meredith. 'Do you like him?'

'Not at all. Not that it matters whether I do or not; but Gerty does not either. I daresay Lord and Lady Gelston think it would be a very good thing.'

'No doubt they do. Nothing more suitable could be devised; and as people of their class usually believe that human affairs are strictly regulated according to their convenience, and look upon Providence as a kind of confidential and trustworthy agent, more or less adroit, but entirely in their interests, no doubt they have it all settled comfortably. There was the complacent ring of such a plan in that pompous old donkey's bray last night, and a kind of protecting mother-in-law-like air about the old woman, which I should not have liked had I been in your sister's place.'

Eleanor's cheek flushed; the tone, even more than the words, told upon her.

'What detestable impertinence!' she said. 'The idea of people who are held to be nobler than others making such calculations, and condescending to such meanness for money!'

'Not in the least surprising; as you will find when you know the world a little better. That the wind should be tempered to the shorn lambs of the aristocracy by the intervention of commoner people's money, they regard as a natural law; and as they are the most irresponsible, they are the most shameless class in society. As to their condescending to meanness for money, you don't reflect—as, indeed, how should you?—that money is the object which best repays such condescension.'

There was a dubious look in Nelly's face. The young girl was flattered and pleased that this handsome accomplished man of the world—who was so much more *her* friend, in consequence of their association in London, than her sister's—should talk to her thus, giving her the benefit of his experience; and yet there might be something to be said, if not for Mr. Dort's parents, for Mr. Dort himself. Her colour deepened, as she said timidly,

'How well *you* must know the world, to be able to discern people's motives and see through their schemes so readily! But perhaps Mr. Dort really cares for Gertrude.'

'Perhaps he does. She is a nice girl; and if her fortune and position don't spoil her, any man might well "care for her," as you call it, for herself. But the disinterestedness of Mr. Dort is not affected, to my mind, by the fact that the appendage to the fortune he is hunting does not happen to be disagreeable. Supposing she had not the fortune, or supposing she lost it, would Mr. Dort care for—that is, marry—your sister then?'

'I don't suppose he would,' said Eleanor thoughtfully.

'And I am sure he would not,' said Meredith. Then, as there was a general rising and dispersion of the company, he added in a whisper, and with a glance beneath which the girl's eyes fell, 'The privilege of being loved for herself is the proudest any woman can boast, and cannot be included in an entail.'

'Mr. M'Ilwaine wants to see you for half an hour, Gertrude, before he returns to Glasgow,' said Haldane Carteret to his niece as she was leaving the breakfast-room, accompanied by Nelly and two young ladies who formed part of the 'staying company' at the Deane.

'Does he?' said Gertrude. 'What for? It won't take me half an hour to bid him good-bye.'

'Business, my dear, business,' said her uncle. 'You are a woman of business now, you know, and must attend to it.'

'I wonder how often I have had notice of *that* fact,' said Gerty. 'I will go to Mr. M'Ilwaine now, uncle; but you must come too, please.—And, Nelly, will you take all the people to the croquet-ground? I will come as soon as I can.'

Gertrude went away with her uncle, and Nelly led the way to an anteroom, in which garden-hats and other articles of casual equipment were to be found.

'It is to be hoped Captain Carteret will not keep on reminding Miss Baldwin of her duties and dignities,' whispered Meredith to Eleanor, as the party assembled on the terrace. 'It will be embarrassing if he does, though she carries it off well, with her pretty air of unconsciousness.'

Eleanor said nothing in answer, but her face darkened, and the first sentence she spoke afterwards had a harsh tone in it.

The day was very fine, the summer heat was tempered by a cool breeze, and the glare of the sun was softened by flitting fleecy clouds. The group collected on the beautifully-kept croquet-ground of the Deane was as pretty and as picturesque as any which was to be seen under the summer sky that day. Mrs. Haldane Carteret, who was by no means 'a frisky matron,' but who enjoyed unbroken animal spirits and much better health than she could have been induced to acknowledge, was particularly fond of croquet, which, as her feet and ankles were irreproachable, was not to be wondered at. She was an indefatigable, a perfectly good-humoured player, and owed not a little of her popularity in the neighbourhood to her ever-ready willingness to get up croquet-parties at home, or to go out to them.

Haldane too was not a bad or a reluctant player; and, on the whole, the Deane held a creditable place in the long list of country houses much devoted to this popular science.

Miss Congreve and her sister 'perfectly doated on' croquet, and all the young men were enthusiasts in the art, except George Ritherdon, who played too badly to like it, and had never gotten over the painful remembrance of having once caused a young lady, whose face was fairer than her temper, to weep tears of spite and wrathfulness by his blunders in a 'match.'

'How long is this going to last?' George asked Meredith, when the game was fairly inaugurated, and the animation of the party

proved how much to their taste their proceedings were.

Meredith did not answer until he had
watched with narrow and critical interest
the stroke which Nelly was then about to
make. When the ball had rolled through
the hoop, and it was somebody else's turn,
he said,

'Until such time as, having breakfasted
at twelve with the prospect of dining at
seven, we can contrive to fancy that we
want something to eat, I suppose.'

'Well, then, as I don't play, and cannot
flatter myself I shall be missed, I shall go
in, write some letters, and have a stroll.
You will tell Miss Baldwin I don't play
croquet, if she should do me the honour to
remark my absence?'

' Certainly,' said Meredith ; and as
George turned away, he said to Eleanor,

'I will tell your sister, if she likes, that

George does not play croquet or any other game.'

She looked up inquiringly.

'No,' he said; 'he is the most thoroughly honest—indeed, I might say the only thoroughly honest — man, who has not any brains, of my acquaintance. *He* won't lay siege to the heiress, and have no eyes for anybody else, no matter how superior; and yet a little or a good deal of money would be as valuable to George as to most men, I believe.'

'I thought Mr. Ritherdon seemed very much taken with Gertrude,' said Nelly, who had ceased for the moment to perform the mystic evolutions of the noble game—in a confidential tone, into which she had unconsciously dropped when speaking to Meredith.

'No doubt, so he is; but if she imagines he is going to be an easy conquest—to propose and be rejected—she will be mistaken.'

A little while ago, and who would have dared to speak in such a tone of her sister to Eleanor Baldwin? Whom would she have believed, who should have told her that she could have heard unmoved insinuations almost amounting to accusations of that sister's vanity, pride, and coquetry? The sweet poison of flattery was taking effect, the deadly plant of jealousy was taking ready root.

'I suppose,' she said, 'every man who comes to the house will be set down as a *prétendant* of Gertrude's—that is to be expected. If any man of our acquaintance has real self-respect, he will keep away.'

'Indeed!' said Meredith. 'Would you make no exceptions to so harsh a rule?—not in favour of those to whom Miss Baldwin would be nothing, except your sister?'

'Nelly, Nelly, what are you about? You are moonstruck, I think!' exclaimed Mrs. Haldane Carteret, whose superabundant alertness could not brook an interval in the game; and Eleanor was absolved by this direct appeal from any necessity to take notice of the words spoken by Meredith.

No immediate opportunity of again addressing Eleanor arose, so Meredith divided his attentions, in claiming her due share of which Mrs. Carteret was very exacting, among the party in general, which was shortly reinforced by the arrival of a number of visitors from the 'contagious countries,' and, conspicuous among them, Mr. Dort. This honourable young gentleman, though all his parents and friends could possibly desire, in point of fashion, was perhaps a little less than people in general might have desired in point of brains. Indeed, he possessed as little of that important ingredient in the composition of humanity as was at all consistent with his keeping up his animal life and keeping himself out of an idiot asylum.

In appearance he was rather prepossessing; for he had a well-bred not-too-pretty face, 'nice' hair (and a capital valet, who rarely received his wages), a tolerably good figure, and better taste in dress than is usually combined with fatuity. He never talked much, which was a good thing for himself and his friends. He had a dim kind of notion that he did not get at his ideas, or at any rate did not put them in words, with quite so much facility as other people did, and so, actuated by a feeble gleam of common sense, he remained tolerably silent in general. As he naturally enjoyed the aristocratic privilege of not being required to exert himself for anybody's good or convenience, he experienced no sort of awkwardness or misgiving when, on making a call, after the ordinary greeting of civilised life (with all the *r*'s eliminated, and all the words jumbled together), he remained perfectly silent, in contemplation of the chimneypiece, except when a dog was present, then he pulled its ears, until the conclusion of his visit. He was very harmless, except to tradespeople, and not unamiable—rather cheerful and happy indeed than otherwise, though his habitual expression was one of vapid discontent. He would have made it sardonic if he could, but he couldn't; he had too little nose and not enough moustache for that, and his strong-minded mamma had advised him to give it up.

'I know your cousin Adolphus does it,' Lady Gelston said indulgently; 'but just consider his natural advantages. Don't do it, Matthew ; you *can't* sneer with an upper lip like yours; and, besides, why *should* you sneer?'

'There's something in that, ma'am, certainly,' returned her admiring son, with his usual deliberation. 'I really don't see why I should; because, you see, I ain't clever enough for people to expect it:' which was the cleverest thing the Honourable Matthew had ever said, up to that period of his existence.

The young ladies in the neighbourhood rather liked Mr. Dort. He was a good deal in Scotland, chiefly because he found an alarming scarcity of ready money was apt to set in, after he had made a comparatively short sojourn in London, and each time this happened he would remark to his friends, in the tone and with the manner of a discoverer,

'And there are things one *must* have money for, don't you know? one can't tick for everything—cabs, and waiters, and so on, don't you know?'

This unhappy perversity of circumstances brought the Honourable Matthew home to his ancestral castle earlier, and caused him to remain there longer, than was customary with the territorial magnates; and Lord and Lady Gelston were, also for sound pecuniary reasons, all-the-year-rounders, and very good neighbours with every family entitled to that distinction. The young ladies, then, liked Mr. Dort. He was useful, agreeable, and 'safe.' Now this peculiar-sounding qualification was one which, however puzzling to the uninitiated, was thoroughly understood in the neighbourhood, and its general acceptation made things very pleasant.

The young ladies might like Mr. Dort, and Mr. Dort might and did like the young ladies, without any risk of undue expectations being excited, or female jealousies and rivalries being aroused. Every one

knew that Mr. Dort's parents intended
their son to marry an heiress, and that
Mr. Dort himself was quite of their opinion. When the appointed time and the
selected heiress should come, the young
ladies were prepared to give up Mr. Dort
with cheerfulness. Perhaps they hoped the
chosen heiress might be ugly, and certainly
they hoped she would 'behave properly to
the neighbourhood,' but there their single-
minded cogitations stopped. A good deal
of the feudal spirit lingered about the Gelston precincts, and if the son of the lord
and the lady, the heir of the undeniably
grand, if rather out-at-elbows, castle, had
been a monk, or a married man, he could
hardly have been more secure from a
design on the part of any young lady to
convert herself into the Honourable Mrs.
Dort.

The pleasantest unanimity of feeling

prevailed in the community respecting him, and all the married ladies declared they 'quite felt for dear Lady Gelston,' in her natural anxiety to 'have her son settled.' Her son was not particularly anxious about it himself, but then it was not his way to be particularly anxious about anything but the 'sit' of his garments, and the punctuality of his meals, and this indifference was normal. Local heiresses were not plentiful in the vicinity of Gelston, but Lady Gelston did not trust to the home supply. She had long ago enlisted the sympathies and the services of such of her friends as enjoyed favourable opportunities for 'knowing about that sort of thing,' and who either had no sons, or such as were happily disposed of. She was a practically-minded woman, and fully alive to the advantage of securing as many resources as possible.

Lady Gelston would have been perfectly capable of the insolence of considering her son's success in the case of the local heiresses—*par excellence*, Miss Baldwin — perfectly indubitable, but of the folly she was not capable. He would have a very good chance, she felt convinced, and she was determined he should try it as soon as it would be decently possible for him to do so.

'Matt is not the only young man of rank she will meet, even here,' said the lady, when she condescended to explain her views to her acquiescent lord.

Who, be it observed, was quite as well convinced of the advantages of the alliance, and quite as anxious it should take place, as his wife; but who preferred repose to action, gave her ladyship credit for practical ability and a contrary taste, and entertained a general idea that scheming in all

its departments had better be left to a woman.

'Matt's chance will be before she goes
to London,' continued her ladyship; 'and
I really think it is a good one. She likes
him, and that goes a great way with a
girl'—said as if she were gently compas-
sionating a weakness—'and I think the
Carterets are sensible people, likely to see
their own advantage in her marrying into
a family who are on good terms with them,
and can make it worth their while to behave nicely. Then there's the advantage *to
her* of the connection. Our son, my dear,
living *here*, is a better match for her than
Lord Anybody's son, living elsewhere, and
unconnected with her people. Really, nothing could be more—more providential,
I really consider it, for her.' And Lady
Gelston nodded approvingly, as if the
power alluded to had been present, and

could have appreciated the polite encouragement.

'Well, my dear, you seem to have taken everything into consideration, and I have no doubt you are right. I hope *they* will see it in the same light.'

'I hope so; but if they don't—and that's why I am anxious Matt should not lose time'—Lady Gelston had a trick of parenthesis—'I shall see about that Treherne girl—Mrs. Peile's niece, you know. Lady John Tarbett sent me a very satisfactory account of her the other day. And by the bye, that reminds me I must go and answer her letter.'

Had Lady Gelston been conscious that all her acquaintances were thoroughly aware of the projects which she cherished in reference to Gertrude Baldwin, she would not have been in the least annoyed. The matter presented itself to her mind in a practical common-sense aspect, much as his designs with regard to the 'middle-aged lady' presented themselves to the mind of Mr. Peter Magnus. 'Husband on one side, wife on the other;' fortune on one side, rank on the other; mutual accommodation, excellent arrangement for all parties—a little condescending on the part of the Honourable Matthew perhaps, but then the girl was really very rich, and that was all about it. Any one ordinarily clear-sighted, and with any knowledge of the world at all, *must* recognise the advantages to all parties. If the Carterets and Miss Baldwin were insensible to them—well, it would be provoking, but there were other heiresses, and certain conditions of heiress-ship were tolerably frequent, in which an Honourable Matthew would be a greater prize than to Miss Meriton Baldwin of the Deane.

When Mr. Dort made his appearance on the Deane croquet-ground, there was not an individual present who did not know that he was there with a definite purpose, and in obedience to the orders of Lady Gelston, and they all watched his proceedings with curiosity. The fates were not propitious to the Honourable Matthew, who had been preparing, on his way, certain pretty speeches, which he flattered himself would be effective, and would help towards 'getting it over,' which was his periphrastic manner of alluding, in his self-communings, to the proposal appointed to be made to Miss Baldwin. Gertrude was not present, and everybody was intent upon croquet.

'Where is your sister?' he asked Eleanor, after they had exchanged good-morrows, and agreed that the ball of the previous night had been a successful festivity.

The droll directness of the question was too much for Nelly; she laughed outright.

'I really cannot tell you,' she replied; 'she ought to have been here long ago; but no doubt she will come now.'

'I hope so,' said Mr. Dort with fervent seriousness. 'I should think she would soon come.'

And then he retired modestly to a garden-seat and softly repeated the phrases, which he began to find it desperately difficult to retain in his memory.

Robert Meredith had adhered with some tenacity to the croquet-party, and had been a witness to this little scene. The amusement, just a little dashed with pique, which Eleanor displayed did not escape him.

'He is an original, certainly,' said Meredith, 'which, for the sake of humanity, it is to be hoped will not be extensively copied. I fancy he will propose to-day.'

'Very likely,' said Nelly; 'every one knows he, or his mother, has intended it for a long time. In fact, Gerty rather wants to have it over, as Mr. Dort is not a bad creature, and the sooner he understands that, though she has no notion of marrying him, he may come here all the same, the pleasanter it will be for all parties.'

'Of course she *has* no notion of marrying him?'

'Mr. Meredith, you are insulting! Gerty marry Matt Dort—an idiot like that!'

'An idiot with an old title and a castle to match, in not distant perspective, combination of county influence, &c. &c. &c.,' said Meredith, smiling; 'not so very improbable, after all.'

'So Lady Gelston thinks,' replied Nelly; ' and won't it be a sell—the slang is delightfully expressive—when she finds it is not he.'

'And wouldn't it be a sell for her lady-ship if it were?' thought Meredith.

'I suppose it will, indeed,' was his reply. 'Though all this is very amusing, I fancy I should consider it very humiliating if I were a woman. I cannot see anything enviable in a position which exposes one to such barefaced speculation.'

'Nonsense!' returned Eleanor, with a forced smile; 'depend on it, if you were a woman, you would like very well to be in Gertrude's position, and have every one making much of you.'

As she spoke she threw down her mallet, and declared herself tired of croquet.

'Here is Gertrude at last,' said Mrs. Haldane Carteret, and all the party looked in the direction of the house. There was Gertrude, coming along the terrace, and with her George Ritherdon, supporting on his arm Mr. Dugdale.

' Let us go and meet them,' said Eleanor, ' and tell Gerty to put the Honourable Matthew out of pain as soon as possible.'

' He is to be here this evening, I suppose,' said Meredith, as they moved off the croquet-ground.

' Yes,' answered Eleanor ; ' Lady Gelston carefully provided for that last night —not that it was necessary, for he would have invited himself, and come under .any circumstances.'

When Eleanor and Meredith joined Miss Baldwin and her escort, George Ritherdon said to his friend :

' I will ask you to take my place. I find the post-hour here is horribly early, and I must really let my mother know where I am.'

' What on earth have you been doing ?'

said Meredith, as he offered his arm to Mr. Dugdale. 'You went away two hours ago to write letters, you said.'

'I think we are to blame,' said Gerty. 'Mr. Ritherdon found us in the morning room—found uncle James and me, I mean —and we got talking, as Miss Congreve says, and—'

'And I had an opportunity of finding out how much Ritherdon is to be liked,' interposed Mr. Dugdale, George being now out of hearing. 'I congratulate you on your companion, Robert.'

Meredith replied cordially, and the party advanced towards the lawn. The two girls preceded Mr. Dugdale and Meredith, and as the sound of their voices reached the latter, he correctly divined that they were amusing themselves at the expense of Mr. Dort. On the approach of Miss Baldwin, the Honourable Matthew promptly abandoned the garden bench, from which no blandishments had previously availed to entice him, and repeated the phrases which had occasioned him so much trouble, with very suspicious glibness, to the undisguised amusement of the two girls. Mr. Dort was not in the least abashed. He had no sense of humour and not a particle of bashfulness, and, if he had reasoned on the subject at all, would have imputed their hilarity to the natural propensity of women to giggle, rather than have entertained any suspicion that he had made himself ridiculous. But he never reasoned, and he was always perfectly comfortable.

The afternoon passed merrily away, and a pleasant dinner-party succeeded. George Ritherdon had become quite a popular person before the promised dance—not at all splendid, in comparison with the ball of the preceding evening—began, and he confided

to Meredith his surprise at finding himself
'getting on so well,' he who was such a
bad hand at 'society business.'

Gertrude gave him several dances that
evening,—Miss Congreve thought rather
too many,—and she gave Mr. Dort one,
and a tolerably prolonged audience in the
ante-room, after which it was generally observed that the expression of discontent
habitual to his features was more marked
than usual. He left the Deane long before
the party broke up, and found his lady
mother still up, and ready to receive his
report of proceedings.

'Well, Matt, how have you got on?'
was her ladyship's terse question.

'I haven't got on at all,' replied the
Honourable Matthew. 'She said "No" almost before I'd asked her, and was so infer-
nally pleasant about it, that, hang it! I
couldn't get up anything like the proper

thing under the circumstances,—you know, mother,—the "may not time—can you not give me a hope?" business.'

'Excessively provoking,' said Lady Gelston, turning very red in the face, and speaking in a tone which was the peculiar aversion of her son: 'she is a stupid perverse girl, and I'm certain you mismanaged the affair.'

'No, I didn't,' said the Honourable Matt; 'there ain't much management about it, that I can see. I said, "Will you marry me?"—that's flat, I think,—and she said, "Certainly not;" *that's* flat, I think;—a perfect flounder, in my opinion.'

'Well, well, it can't be helped,' said Lady Gelston, with a glance at her son which might have meant that she had arrived at a comprehension of what a fool he really was. 'There, go away, and let me get to bed. It's too bad; but there's no help for it. We must only try elsewhere,' she continued, as if speaking to herself.

'Stop a bit, mother,' interposed the Honourable Matt, without the least impatience or any change of expression, 'I want to consult you about something. Don't you think what I particularly want is ready money—money that isn't tied up, I mean— not the entail business, don't you know, but the other thing?'

'I think you want money in any way and in any quantity in which it can be had,' returned Lady Gelston impatiently. 'How can you ask such foolish questions?'

'I'm not. I heard all about Nelly Baldwin's money to-night. Captain Carteret was talking about it to old Largs, and he's so deaf that the Captain had to roar all the particulars; and I'll tell you what, mother, —by Jove, I'll go in for Nelly.'

Robert Meredith and George Ritherdon were to remain a week at the Deane. The three days which succeeded their arrival were passed in the ordinary pleasurable pursuits of a luxurious and hospitable country-house, and were unmarked by any events which made themselves at all conspicuous. Nevertheless they were days with a meaning, an epoch with a history, and their course included two incidents. The sisters had a quarrel, which they kept strictly to themselves; and George Ritherdon received a long letter, which he read with profound amazement, which he promptly destroyed, and concerning whose contents he said not a word to any one.

CHAPTER VI.

THE FIRST MOVES IN THE GAME.

SOME time passed away, after the memorable fête which had celebrated the majority of Miss Meriton Baldwin of the Deane, during which, to an uninitiated observer, the aspect of affairs in that splendid and well-regulated mansion remained unchanged. County festivities took place; and the importance of the young ladies at the Deane was not a better established fact than their popularity.

With the comic seriousness which distinguished him, the Honourable Matthew Dort had 'gone in for Nelly.' He visited at the Deane with tranquil regularity, he

played croquet imperturbably; only that
he now watched Eleanor's balls, and was
as confident she would 'croquet' everybody
as he had formerly been free from doubt
about Gertrude's prowess; he rehearsed his
speeches, and uttered them with entire self-
possession.   In due time he proposed to
Eleanor, in the exact terms in which he
had already done Gertrude that honour;
and he was refused by her quite as defini-
tively, but less politely than he had been
refused by her sister. On this occasion also
he went home to his mother, and related
to her his defeat with a happy absence of
embarrassment.

Lady Gelston was very angry.   She
really did not know what the world—and
especially the young women who were in
it—was coming to; she wondered who the
Baldwin girls expected to get.   But of one
thing she was convinced—Matthew must

have made a fool of himself somehow, or
he could not have failed in both instances.
The accused Matthew did not defend himself. Very likely he had made a fool of
himself, but it could not be helped. Neither
Gertrude nor Eleanor would marry him,
and it was quite clear he could not make
either of them do so. His mother had much
better not worry herself about them ; and
when the shooting was over, or he was tired
of it, he would ' look-up that girl of Lady
Jane Tarbert's.'

With this prospect, and with the intention of snubbing the Baldwins, Lady Gelston was forced to be content. But the
snubbing, though her ladyship was an adept
in the practice, did not succeed. The Baldwins declined to perceive that they were
snubbed, and the neighbourhood declined
to follow Lady Gelston's lead in this particular. The Deane was the most popular

house in the county, and the Baldwins were
the happiest and most enviable people.

This fair surface was but a deceitful
seeming; at least, so far as the sisters were
concerned. An estrangement, which had
had its commencement on Gertrude's birthday, and had since increased by insensible
degrees, had grown up between them; an
estrangement which not all their efforts—
made in the case of Eleanor from pride,
in that of Gertrude from wounded feeling
—could hide from the notice of their uncle
and aunt, from James Dugdale and Rose
Doran; an estrangement which made each
eagerly court external associations, and find
relief, in the frequent presence of others,
from the constant sense of their changed
relation. James Dugdale saw this change
with keen sorrow; but when he attempted
to investigate it, he was met by Gertrude
with an earnest assurance that she was en-

tirely ignorant of its origin, and an equally earnest entreaty that he would not speak to Eleanor about it. It would be useless, Gertrude said, and she must put her faith in time and her sister's truer interpretation of her.

Appeal to Eleanor was met with flat denial, and an angry refusal to submit to interference, which in itself betrayed the evil root of all this dissension. Gertrude was supreme, the angry sister said; *she* was nothing. Gertrude of course could not err; all the good things of this world were for Gertrude, including the absolute subservience of her sister. But she might not, indeed she should not, find it quite so easy to command *that*. A good deal of harm was done by Mrs. Carteret, not intentionally, but yet after her characteristic fashion. She much preferred Eleanor to Gertrude, and she made herself a partisan of the former, by pitying her, because *she* only could know how little she was really to blame. Haldane treated the matter very lightly. He regarded it as a girlish squabble, which would resolve itself into nothing in a very short time, and at the worst would be dissipated by a stronger feeling. So soon as a lover should appear on the scene, their good-humoured uncle believed it would be all right,—provided indeed they did not happen to fall in love with the same man, and quarrel desperately about him.

Rose Doran regarded the state of things with anger and horror.

'It's just the devil's work, sir,' she said to Mr. Dugdale; 'puttin' jealousy and bitterness between them two, fatherless and motherless as they are, and no one to show them the only kind of love in which there's no room for more or less. It's just the devil's work, and he's doing it bravely; and

Miss Nelly's to his hand, for that jealousy was always in her; not but there's somebody behindhand, I'm sure of it, puttin' coals on the fire.'

Rose was at first disposed to suspect Mrs. Carteret of this supererogatory work, but she did not continue to suspect her. She knew the girls so thoroughly, she was in no doubt respecting the amount of influence their aunt could exert over them, and in Nelly's case she was aware this was much less than in that of Gertrude. Besides, Mrs. Doran's practical wisdom controlled her feminine suspicion; she could not discern an adequate motive, and she therefore exonerated aunt Lucy. But she was no less convinced that, in this unhappy matter, Eleanor was not left alone to the unassisted promptings of her disposition, in which Rose had early perceived the terrible taint of jealousy. And her acute observa-

tion guided her aright before long; it guided
her to an individual whom she had instinctively distrusted in his boyhood—to Robert
Meredith.

Though she had hardly seen him for
many years past, and though, in her position in the household at the Deane, she had
not come into any contact with him of late,
Rose Doran had never got over the dislike
of Robert Meredith which she had conceived
at the terrible time of her beloved mistress's
death.   On that occasion James Dugdale
had obeyed Margaret's instructions so faithfully and promptly, that Rose Moore had
reached the Deane in time to kneel beside
her unclosed coffin, and whisper, on her
cold lips, the promise on which she had
instinctively relied,—the promise that her
children should be henceforth Rose's sacred
charge and care.   Among the mourners at
the funeral of Mrs. Baldwin were Hayes

Meredith and his son; the former entirely absorbed in grief for the event, and in thoughts of the future, as his secret knowledge forced him to contemplate it; the latter, with ample leisure of mind to look about him, to observe and admire, and with the pleasant conviction that every one was too much occupied to take any notice of him. He conducted himself with propriety at the funeral, and afterwards, while he was in sight of the family; and he was far from supposing that Rose Moore was watching his looks and his manner, on other occasions, with mingled disgust and curiosity, and that she said to herself, ' The Lord be good to us! but I believe, upon my soul and faith, *the boy is glad she's taken.*'

Rose had never deliberately recalled this impression during all the years which had witnessed her faithful fulfilment of her vow, but she had never lost it; and the conviction which now came to her, during Robert Meredith's stay at the Deane, and which gained strength with every day which ensued on his departure, had its origin in it. Had it needed confirmation, it would have obtained it from the utter and peremptory rejection of her good offices, on Nelly's part, and the burst of angry disdain with which the infatuated girl met her suggestion, that Mr. Meredith was no friend of Gertrude's. Eleanor Baldwin had travelled no small distance on the thorny road of evil, when she rewarded Rose's suggestion with a haughty request, which fired Rose's Irish blood, but with a flame quickly quenched in healing waters of love and pity,—that she would in future remember, and keep, *her place.*

'It's because I never forget my place, the place your mother put me in, Miss Nelly, that I warn you,' said her faithful friend.

Then Eleanor felt ashamed of herself; but pride and anger and deadly jealousy carried the day over the wholesome sentiment, and she turned away hastily, leaving Rose without a word.

In much more than its external meaning was that festival time of deep importance to Gertrude and Eleanor Meriton Baldwin. It was fraught with the fate of both. While Robert Meredith and his friend remained at the Deane, the relation of the sisters was unchanged in appearance. It seemed as if their mysterious quarrel had had no lasting effect. The after estrangement was, however, its legitimate fruit, as well as the consequence of the pernicious ideas which Robert Meredith had set himself assiduously to cultivate in the mind of Nelly. An explanation of the state of mind of Robert Meredith, at the termination of his visit to the Deane, will sufficiently elucidate the ·

quarrel of the sisters, and its distressing results.

Robert Meredith had arrived at the Deane full of one purpose, which had been vaguely present to his mind for some years, but to which certain circumstances had of late lent consistency, fixedness, and urgency. This purpose was to make himself acceptable in the eyes of Miss Baldwin. He had hitherto troubled himself but little about the young lady. When she should have reached her majority, his time should have come. It had arrived; and not Mr. M'Ilwaine himself—who had gone to the Deane, accompanied by the huge mass of papers to which Haldane Carteret had found it difficult to induce his niece to give reasonable attention—had proceeded thither with a more strictly business-like purpose in view than that which actuated the handsome barrister. Robert would have despised himself as sin-

cerely, and almost as much, as he was in
the habit of despising his neighbours, if he
had been capable of permitting sentiment
to influence him in so grave an affair as
that of securing his fortune for life,—which
was precisely his purpose ; and he had
formed his plans totally irrespective of Gertrude's attractions, or their possible influence upon himself. He had two schemes
in his mind, both, in his belief, equally
practicable; and he determined to be guided
by circumstances as to which of the two he
should adopt. If the second should present itself as the more advisable, an indispensable preliminary to the secure playing
of the long game it would involve was the
alienation of the sisters. It could do no
harm, in any case, to make an immediate
move in that direction ; and therefore Robert Meredith made it.

When Eleanor Baldwin made her escape

from the ballroom on that memorable night, leaving her sister to the cares which her superior importance devolved upon her, Robert Meredith's eager words of admiration, and still more expressive looks, had filled the girl's heart—already dangerously trembling towards him — with a strange tumultuous joy, contending with the jealous bitterness he had contrived to implant in it.   But when he and George Ritherdon bade one another good-night at the door of George's room, after a brief commentary upon the beauty of the morning, he had enough that was ever in his thoughts to keep him from sleep.   The comparative advantages of the first of his plans over the second had immensely increased in his estimation.

The beauty, the simplicity, the tender pathetic grace of Gertrude, had struck with a strange attractive freshness upon his palled sense, and he had awakened, with a delicious consciousness, to the conviction that he might combine the utmost gratification of two passions by the successful prosecution of his scheme. To make that delicate, refined, lovely girl love him as passionately, as foolishly, as the dark beauty, her sister, would love him, if it suited his purpose to encourage the dawning feeling he had seen in her eyes, and felt in every movement and word of hers during the evening, would indeed be triumph, adding a delicious flavour to the wealth and station which should be his. He understood now what the charm was which Gertrude's mother, whom he had hated, had had for men, —the charm of a pure and refined intellectuality, with underlying possibilities of intense and exalted feeling,—these were to be divined in the depths of the clear gray, unabashed eyes, and in the sensitive curves of a mouth as delicate as her mother's, but less ascetic.

Had he made a favourable impression on Gertrude? Had she learned from her sister's report to regard him with favour, and had he confirmed that report? He did not feel comfortably certain on this point. Gertrude had not given him any indication beyond the additional attention which he claimed as Mr. Dugdale's particular friend. But Robert Meredith did not trouble himself much on this point; he had time before him, and he knew perfectly well how to use it. But it was characteristic of the man that, though he dwelt, to his last waking moment, upon Gertrude's beauty and charm, he thought, just as he fell asleep, 'If she thwarts me, it will all add zest to the revenge which Miss Eleanor's eyes tell me is secure in any case.'

The story of the remainder of Robert

Meredith's visit may be briefly told. Gertrude did thwart him. Not intentionally; for she, being the most candid of girls, was wholly incapable of understanding his double-dealing policy. She frankly regarded him as her sister's admirer, and she unreservedly regretted that he should be so. She did not like Robert Meredith; between him and her there was an absolute absence of sympathy, and she shrank with an inexplicable repugnance and fear from his looks —covert and yet bold—and from the admiration which he insinuated, the understanding which he attempted to imply, whenever he could take or contrive an opportunity of doing so, unobserved and unheard by Eleanor. She avoided him whenever it was possible, and she never remained alone with him.

Robert Meredith was a vain man—but vanity was not his ruling passion, one or two others had precedence of it—therefore he did not fail to see, or hesitate to confess to himself, that Gertrude had thwarted him, that there would not be room, in the accomplishment of his scheme, for the delicious gratification of two passions at once, and that he would do well to fall back upon the second game, for playing which he had the cards in his hand. It was not without intense mortification he made this avowal to himself. He was a man to whom failure was indeed bitter; but he speedily found consolation in musing upon the perfection of a certain revenge which he meditated.

'If she would marry me, in ignorance,' he said to himself, 'I should be the Deane's master and hers; but, if she would not marry me under any circumstances, to escape any penalty—and I begin to think that is certain now—I have her in my power, and *all, all, all* will be mine.'

These reflections, made by Robert Meredith during the week which was to conclude his stay at the Deane, led him to take a certain resolution, whose execution was fraught with immediate results to the sisters.

A small but very animated dancing-party had taken place at the Deane; and Robert had closely studied the demeanour of Gertrude and Eleanor to him and to each other. The estrangement of the sisters had not then become manifest; but he detected and exulted in it. On Gertrude's part there was a nervous anxiety to put Eleanor forward, to consult her, to defer to her in everything; on Eleanor's there was an affectation of indifference, an assumption of deference, a giving of herself the appearance of being a guest, which was in extremely bad taste, but thoroughly delightful to Robert Meredith. If a servant asked Eleanor a question, she pointedly referred him to her sister ; she professed an entire ignorance of Miss Baldwin's plans for the evening; she divided herself from her in innumerable little expressive ways, which Gertrude noted with a sick heart and a manner which betrayed painful nervousness ; and she abandoned herself to the influence of the flattery and the insidious suggestions of the tempter to a degree which justified him in believing that he might be entirely sure of her, whether the pursuit of his purpose should lead him to break her heart by marrying her sister, or crown her hopes by marrying herself.

It was Gertrude's custom to resort to the library every morning after breakfast, and there to occupy herself with her drawing, at a table beside a large window which

opened on the lawn. She was usually undisturbed, as Mr. Dugdale remained in his
own rooms all the morning, her uncle frequented the stable and farmyard, Eleanor
devoted the morning hours to music, and
Mrs. Carteret had no attraction towards
the library. George Ritherdon had sometimes found his way thither ; and Gertrude
had, on those occasions, found it not unpleasant to lay aside her pencil, and discuss
with her guest some of the contents of her
amply - stored bookshelves. But George
was engaged in writing letters on the morning which followed the before-mentioned
dancing-party; and Robert Meredith found
Miss Baldwin, as he expected, alone. Gertrude tried hard to receive him in the
most ordinary way, but her embarrassment was distressingly apparent ; and he
coolly showed her that he perceived it.
After a few words—she could hardly have

told what words—she collected her drawing-materials, and said something confusedly about being waited for by Mrs. Carteret, as she rose to leave the room. But Robert Meredith, with a bold fixed look, which, in spite of herself, she saw and felt in every nerve, detained her; and gravely informing her that he had purposely selected that opportunity of finding her alone, in order to make a communication of importance to her, requested her to listen to him. His manner was not loverlike, it was even, under all the formality of his address, slightly contemptuous; but she knew instantly what it was she had to listen to, and a prayer arose in her heart by a sudden inexplicable impulse. She resumed her seat, and leaning her arm on the table which divided her from Robert Meredith, she shaded her eyes with her hand, and prepared to listen to him.

It was as her instinctive dread had told her. In set phrase, and with his bold covetous eyes fixed upon her, Meredith told her his errand, — told her he loved her, and asked her to marry him — made mention too of her wealth, and the risk he ran of being misinterpreted by the world, of having base motives imparted to him— a risk more than counterbalanced by his love, and his faith in his ability to make her understand and believe that she was sought by him for herself alone.

Robert Meredith spoke well, and with fire and energy; but, as Gertrude listened to him, her distress and embarrassment subsided, and she removed the sheltering hand from her eyes. When he urgently entreated her to reply, she said very gently:

'I should feel more pain, Mr. Meredith, in telling you that I cannot return the preference with which you honour me, if I did not feel so convinced that your love for me is only imaginary. Had it been real, you would not have remembered my wealth, or cared about the opinion of the world.'

This answer staggered the man to whom it was addressed more than any indignation could have done. He burst out into renewed protestations; but Gertrude, with grave dignity, begged him to desist, and again asserting that as her guardian's friend he should ever be esteemed hers, assured him it was useless to pursue his suit. Then she rose, and moved towards the door.

'Is this a final answer, Miss Baldwin?' asked Meredith.

'Quite final, Mr. Meredith.'

'Stay a moment. May I hope you will not add to the mortification of this refusal the injury of making it known to Mr. Dugdale or Mrs. Carteret, indeed to any one?

I confess I could hardly endure the ridicule or the compassion which must attend a rejected suitor of the heiress of the Deane.'

There was a devil's sneer in his voice and on his face; but Gerty took no heed of it, as she replied, with quiet dignity,

'We have a code of honour also, we women, Mr. Meredith; and you may be quite sure I shall never so far offend against it as to mention this matter to *any one.*' Then she added, with a sweet smile, in which her perfect incredulity regarding his professions was fully though unconsciously expressed:

'I will leave you now; and I hope you will forget all this as soon and as completely as I shall.'

Robert Meredith followed her with his eyes as she left the room, and passing along the terrace, went down into her flower-garden, and lingered there, utterly oblivious of him; and a deadly feeling of hatred, such hatred as springs most profusely from baffled passion, arose in his heart, and blossomed into sudden strength and purpose.

'Yes,' he muttered; 'you have taken up the thread of your mother's story, and you shall spin it out to some purpose. A little while, and Eleanor will be of age; and then, my fine heiress of the Deane, then we shall see who has won to-day. A little while, and if I can only keep Oakley quiet till then, I am safe. Safe! more than safe, —triumphant, victorious!'

It was on the next day that Nelly, intoxicated by the artful flatteries of Robert Meredith, and tortured by the jealousy which he had fostered, taunted her sister with the powerlessness of money to purchase love. The taunt fell harmlessly on Gertrude's pure and upright heart; but it

startled her, uttered by her sister. How
had Nelly come by such knowledge, and
why did she apply it to her? She hastily
asked her why; and to her astonishment
was answered, that in one treasure at least
Nelly was richer than she was—the treasure of a brave and true man's love! The
reply shook Gertrude like a reed. There
was indeed one man who answered to this
description; there was one man to win
whose love would be the most blissful lot
which Heaven could bestow. There was
one man, who never, by word or deed or
look, had implied to Gertrude Baldwin that
such a lot might be hers—had her sister
won *him?* Well indeed might she exult,
if she were so supremely blest, and hold
not Gertrude only, but all womankind her
inferiors. Pale and breathless, she awaited
the complete elucidation to be expected
from Eleanor's taunting wrath, and it came.

It came, not as her fearful shrinking heart had foreboden, but in the avowal that Eleanor spoke of Robert Meredith.

With the passing away of the great pang of terror that had clutched at her heart, Gertrude was again calm and clear-sighted; but she was deeply grieved. She felt how unworthy was the man her sister loved, how baseless her belief that she possessed his affections. She was far from being able to comprehend such a nature as that of Robert Meredith; but she had a vague consciousness that, in his binding her to secrecy respecting his proposal to her, there had been a treacherous intent; and though she would not break her promise, she appealed to her sister on grounds and terms which a little more knowledge of human nature would have taught her must be in vain. Then came the inevitable result, a bitter and lasting quarrel, and an ineradicable belief on Eleanor's part that Gertrude's refusal to credit Meredith's love for her sister arose from the most despicable motives—pride, envy, and jealousy. Where was the sisterly love, where was the unbroken confidence of years now? Blasted by the fierce breath of passion, poisoned by the insidious art of the tempter.

So a treacherous appearance of calm and happiness existed at the Deane during the months which succeeded the departure of the friends, and none but those concerned were aware of two circumstances which had entirely changed the lives of the bright and beautiful sisters. One was the fact that Eleanor Baldwin was secretly betrothed to Robert Meredith, with the understanding that on her coming of age she would marry him, with or without the consent of her relatives. The other was that the plodding industrious barrister

George Ritherdon, who carried back to his chambers in the Temple more than one unaccustomed sensation, had taken with him, unconsciously, the unasked heart of the young mistress of the Deane.

CHAPTER VII.

DRIFTING.

WITH the commencement of the season, Major and Mrs. Carteret and their nieces followed the multitude to London. This proceeding was but little in accordance with the wishes of Gertrude Baldwin, who loved her home and her dependents, the pleasant routine of her country duties and recreations; but she could not oppose herself to the general opinion that it was the right thing to do, in which even Mr. Dugdale, her great support and ally, agreed with the others. In her capacity of woman of fashion, Mrs. Carteret was quite shocked that Gertrude should have passed her twenty-

first year without coming out in proper
style in London; but in that of chaperone,
or, as she called it, maternal friend to a
great heiress, she had recognised the wisdom
and propriety of permitting her to attain to
years of discretion before she should be
formally delivered over to the wiles of the
fortune-hunters and the perils of the 'great
world.' Not but that there were fortune-
hunters in Scotland, witness the Honourable
Matthew Dort; but Gertrude was not likely
to be bewildered by their devices in the
sober atmosphere of her home.

Miss Baldwin's mind had not changed
on the subject of the superiority of her
Scottish home to anything which a London
residence could offer, and which would certainly wear an air of triumph for her, however false that air might be. Gertrude was
by no means worldly wise. She had none
of the cynical foresight leading her to see

in every one who approached her a covetous
idolater of her wealth. She would have
regarded herself with horror if she had lost
her faith in love or friendship; and indeed
she had been so accustomed to the presence
of wealth all her life, that she did not understand its effect on others, and had no mental
standard by which to estimate its value,
either material or moral. It was not, therefore, from any unwomanly disdain of the
motives of those whom she was to sojourn
amongst in London that Gertrude took the
prospect coolly, showing none of the excitement and exultation to which Eleanor gave
unrestrained expression, and which made
her amiable to Gertrude to an extent un-
paralleled for many months past. The truth
was that there was a secret in Gertrude's
heart, a preoccupation of Gertrude's mind,
to which everything beside, so far as she was
individually concerned, had to yield. This

pervading sentiment did not render her self-
ish, she was as ready with her sympathies
for others as ever, but it did make her
absent and indifferent.

Robert Meredith and his friend had
passed a fortnight at Christmas at the
Deane, and there the plans of the family
for the coming season had been discussed.
Gertrude had learned with surprise and dis-
comfiture that her living in London, where
he lived, would not imply her seeing very
much of George Ritherdon. She fancied
he had been at some pains to make her understand this, and the consciousness rendered her uneasy. Why had he dwelt upon
the busy nature of his life, the diversity between his occupations and hers? Why had
he drawn a merry sketch for her of the
wide difference between the society, such
as it was, in which alone he had a footing,
and the gilded saloons which were to throw

their doors open for her? He had not offended her by cynicism, which was as far from his happy and loyal nature as from hers; but he had made her thoughtful and uncomfortable by an insistance upon this point, which she could but refer to a wish to make her understand that she must not expect him to contribute to the anticipated pleasures of her sojourn in London. And with this conviction vanished all such anticipations from Gertrude's fancy.

That was an enchanted fortnight. The hours had flown, and a beautiful new world had opened itself to the girl's perception. She had been too happy to be afraid of Robert Meredith, or ungracious to him. She had utterly forgotten the rule of action she had laid down for herself, in consideration of her sister's perverse jealousy and alienation. She had determined to treat Meredith with cold politeness, to show him and Eleanor that she imputed to his sinister influence the state of things which occasioned her so much pain. But she forgot the pain; she was happy, and the sunshine of her content spread all around her.

Robert Meredith had a difficult game to play at this time, but he played it with skill and success. It is not a light test of skill when an elderly coquette is persuaded by a *ci-devant* admirer to abandon the conquering for the confidential *rôle*, and this was precisely the test which Robert Meredith applied to his *savoir faire*. The secret betrothal between himself and Eleanor placed them on so secure a footing, that he was able, without annoying Eleanor, notwithstanding her exacting disposition, to devote much of his time to Mrs. Carteret, towards whom his tone modified itself from the slightly vulgar, somewhat obtrusive gallantry which had been wont to characterise it,

to the very perfection of deferential observance and highly-prized intimacy. He had
appealed to some of Eleanor's best feelings
in order to induce her to consent to the
secrecy of their engagement—to her disin-
clination to produce family discord, to her
duty of avoiding the rendering of her aunt's
position as between her and Gertrude difficult, and to her noble confidence in his
judgment and fidelity, which it should be
his loftiest aim in life to justify and re-
ward.

He had not only poisoned Eleanor's
mind against her sister, but he had succeeded in undermining the grateful affection which the misguided girl had once
entertained for Mr. Dugdale. He had made
her remark the preference which, in many
small ways, the old man showed for Gertrude—a preference of whose origin and
justification Eleanor had no knowledge to

enable her to understand it aright—and assured her that in him too, in deference to
that universal baseness which dictated subservience to her sister's wealth, Eleanor
would find a bitter opponent to her love, a
ruthless adversary of her happiness. His
wicked counsels prevailed. Something ro-
mantic in the girl's disposition responded to
the idea of a persecuted passion; and the
demon of jealousy, now thoroughly awakened
in her, wrought unrestrained all the mis-
chief her human evil genius desired. Meredith counselled Eleanor to soften her manner towards Gertrude, for the better security
of their secret against the danger of her
awakened suspicions; and she obeyed him.
He forbade her to tell Mrs. Carteret all the
truth, lest it might hereafter compromise
her with her husband and Mr. Dugdale, but
told her to cultivate her good graces in
every way, so that in the time to come her

aid might be sure; and she obeyed him.
The result of all this was much more peace
for Gertrude; and as Meredith kept himself
out of her way, devoting himself to Mrs.
Carteret and Eleanor, and leaving George
Ritherdon to her society, it had the additional effect of increasing and consolidat-
ing her attachment to George.

Major Carteret was habitually unobserv-
ant; his wife confined her attention to
Robert Meredith, of whose wishes she was
the delighted confidante, and Eleanor, whom
she did not at present suspect of more than
an incipient inclination towards Robert.
Mr. Dugdale,—whose health had declined
considerably since the autumn, did not leave
his rooms, and saw the different members
of the family singly,—was totally unconscious of the drama being played out so
near him. Things were better between the
sisters, and he rejoiced at that. The favour-

able impression which George Ritherdon had made upon him on his first visit to the Deane was deepened during his second, and he greatly enjoyed his society. Gertrude passed many happy hours, working or drawing, beside her old friend's sofa, while the two men talked with mutual pleasure and sympathy. When that happy fortnight ended and the friends had returned to London, Gertrude found her greatest consolation in Mr. Dugdale's frequent allusions to George, and in the eulogiums which he pronounced on his mind and his manners, the latter being a point on which the old gentleman was difficult and fastidious.

During and since that time, Gertrude, who was singularly free from vanity and quite incapable of pretence, had frequently asked herself whether she had not given her heart to one who did not love her. Even if it had been so to her indisputable knowledge, she would not have striven to withdraw the gift. She loved him, once and for ever, and she would sanctify that love in her heart, if he were never to be more to her than the truest and most valued of friends. She was utterly sincere and candid in this resolution; she had no fore-knowledge of the difficulty, the impossibility of maintaining it. She was content, ay, even happy, in her uncertainty, which was sometimes hope, but never despair. Such a possibility as that George should love her and refrain from telling her so, because of her wealth, literally never occurred to her, any more than that, if he loved her, and told her so, the most unscrupulous calumniator in the world could accuse him of caring for that wealth, of even remembering it. It had no place in her thoughts at all. She lived her dream-life happily; sometimes her dreams were brighter, sometimes more sombre; but their glitter did not come from her gold, their shadow was not cast by cynical doubt, by worldly-wise suspicion.

When the time came for their journey to London, Gertrude was more sad than elated. Her best friend, the one on whom she leaned with the trusting reliance of a daughter, from whom she had ever experienced the fond indulgence of a parent, was to remain at the Deane. Mr. Dugdale's health rendered it impossible for him to accompany the family, and Mrs. Carteret and Eleanor did not regret his absence. Their feelings were in accord on every point connected with the expedition. Eleanor foresaw no impediment to her frequent enjoyment of Robert Meredith's society, under the auspices of Mrs. Carteret, who, on her part, had great satisfaction in the prospect of partaking in the gaieties of a London season, for which she still retained an unpalled taste, and maintaining a splendid establishment at the expense of her niece.

More than half the interval which had to elapse between Gertrude's attainment of her majority and Eleanor's reaching a similar period had now elapsed, and Robert Meredith's successful prosecution of his schemes with respect to the Baldwins was uncheckered by any reverse. In other respects things were not progressing quite so favourably with him. He had been negligent in his professional business of late, since his mind had been full of the mysterious game he was playing, and the inevitable, inexorable result of this negligence was making itself felt. George Ritherdon, on the contrary, was getting on rapidly for a barrister, and was beginning to be talked about as a man with a name and a standing. The relations between the two had insensibly relaxed, as was only natural, considering that the strongest tie between them, their common industry, their common ambition, had so considerably slackened. Nothing approaching to a quarrel had taken place; but they were tired of one another, and each was aware of the fact. The sentiment dated from their second visit to the Deane, whence each had returned preoccupied with his own thoughts, his own preferences, and profoundly conscious that no sympathy existed between them.

Little had been said between the two relative to the Baldwins' sojourn in London; and when George Ritherdon, made aware of their arrival by the *Morning Post*, asked his friend when he intended to present himself at their house in Portman-square, he was disagreeably surprised by the cold brevity of Meredith's reply that he had been there already, had indeed seen the ladies on the very day of their arrival, and was going to dine with them the same evening.

George made no remark upon this communication, and left a card for Major Carteret on the following day. An invitation to dinner follotved, and on his mentioning the circumstance to Meredith, George was surprised and offended by his manner. He laughed unpleasantly, and said something about the futility of George's expecting to be received on the same footing as he had been in the country, which made him decidedly angry.

'I don't understand you, Meredith,' he said. 'You brought me to the Deane, I owe the acquaintance entirely to you, and now you talk as if you resented it.'

'Nonsense, old fellow,' returned Robert with good humour, which cost him an effort; 'I only discourage your going to the Baldwins, because I do not want to hear you talked of as an unsuccessful competitor for the heiress's money-bags, and because I know, if you have any leaning in that direction, it will be quite useless. The young ladies fly at higher game than you or I.'

A deep flush overspread George Ritherdon's face as he replied:

'I beg you will not include me, in your own mind, in the category of fortune-hunters; as for what other people think or say, you need not trouble yourself.'

'As you please. I only warn you that Gertrude Baldwin is an interested coquette, determined to make the most of her money, —to buy rank with it, at all events, but by no means averse to numbering her thousands of victims in the mean time.'

'You speak harshly of this girl, Meredith, and cruelly.'

'I speak candidly, because I am speak-

ing to *you*. You don't suppose I would
put another fellow on his guard. I might
have got bit myself, you know, if I had not
understood her in time. However, we had
better not talk about it. Forewarned, fore-
armed, they say, though I can't say I ever
knew any good come of warning any
one.'

Thereupon Meredith pretended to be
very busy with his papers, and the subject
dropped. But it left a very unpleasant impression on George's mind. 'An interested
coquette!' No more revolting description
could be given of any woman within the
category of those whom an honest man
could ever think of marrying. Had George
Ritherdon thought of marrying Gertrude?
No. Did he love her? He knew in his heart
he did; but he did not question for a moment his power of keeping the fact hidden
from the object of his love, and every other

person. He would have regarded the declaration of his feelings to an inexperienced girl, who had had no opportunity of choice, of seeing the world, of forming her judgment of character, to whom the language of love was utterly unknown, on the eve of her entrance upon a scene on which she ought to enter perfectly untrammelled, as in the highest degree dishonourable. He would have held this opinion concerning any woman whose wealth should have made her position so exceptionally difficult as that of Gertrude; but in her particular instance he had an additional motive for his strict self-conquest and reticence, which, if it ever could be explained, must remain concealed for the present.

George Ritherdon had no coxcombry or conceit about him, and he had not made up his mind by any means that Gertrude loved him, or was likely to be brought to

love him in the future, should he find that
the ordeal to which she was about to be
exposed had left her still fancy-free, and
his own circumstances be such as to enable
him to believe he might try for the great
prize of her heart and hand without dis-
honour. He did not deceive himself as to
the obstacles and the rivals he might have
to encounter; he gave all the fascinations
of the new sphere in which Gertrude was
about to shine their full credit and importance, and he contented himself with this
conclusion:

'If, when she has had full experience,
ample time, when she knows her position
and her own mind perfectly, I can be sure
that she prefers me to all the world beside,
I will win her, and marry her, without be-
stowing a thought on her fortune, or caring
a straw for any one's interpretation of my
motives, caring only for *hers.*'

Steadily acting upon the plan he had laid down for himself, George Ritherdon frequented Gertrude's society not often enough to make his visits a subject of comment, not sufficiently seldom to induce her to think him indifferent or estranged. She and Eleanor were going through the ordinary routine of the life of London in the season; he rarely participated in its more tumultuous and irrational pleasures. But he kept a tolerably strict watch upon Gertrude for all that; and he had no reason to believe, at the end of the second month of her stay in London, that any one of the numerous admirers with whom rumour and his own observation had accredited her, had found the slightest favour with the young lady of the Deane.

Before the end of that second month, Robert Meredith and George Ritherdon had parted company. The former could per-

haps have given a plain and conclusive reason for his desire that so it should be; but,
in the case of the latter, the actuating motive was more vague. George felt that they
did not get on together. The Baldwins
were hardly ever mentioned between them,
though each knew the terms on which the
other stood with the family, and they not
unfrequently met at the house in Portman-
square. The dissolution of the old arrangement, once so pleasant to them both, was
plainly imminent to each before it actually
occurred, and it might have come about after a disagreeable fashion but for a fortunate
accident. The gentleman who had been
George's university tutor, and with whom
he had always maintained intimate relations,
died, and bequeathed to George his numerous and valuable library. What was he to
do with the books? Their joint chambers
would not accommodate them. George took

a large set in another building, and the
difficulty was solved, to their mutual relief,
without a quarrel.

The season was a brilliant one, and Gertrude and Eleanor Baldwin had their full
share of its glories and its pleasures. They
enjoyed it, after their different fashions, but
Gertrude more than Eleanor. In the heart
of each there was indeed a disquieting secret; but in the one case there was no self-
reproach, no misgiving, while in the other
that voice would occasionally make itself
heard. As time passed over, Gertrude felt
more and more hopeful that George Ritherdon loved her, though for some reason which
she could not penetrate, but to which it was
not difficult for her docile nature to submit,
he did not at present avow the sentiment.
Her happiness was not lost, it was only de-
ferred; she would be patient, and then she
could always comfort herself with the know-

ledge that her love for him—pure, lofty, with no element of torment in it—could never die, or be taken from her, while she lived.

Eleanor's lot was by no means so favoured, and she proved more difficult to manage than Robert Meredith had foreseen. She chafed under the restraint of her position, and suffered agonies of suspicion and jealousy. The evil passion which he had been quick to see and skilful to cultivate, for his own purposes, was easily turned against him, a contingency which with all his astuteness he had failed to apprehend; and Eleanor's daily increasing imperiousness and distrust made him tremble for the safety of his secret and the success of his plans.

Nothing made Eleanor so suspicious of the falsehood of his professions, nothing exasperated her so much, as Robert Meredith's imperviousness to the feeling which had obtained so fearful a dominion over her. If she could but have roused his jealousy, as she ceaselessly endeavoured to do, by such reckless flirtations as brought her into trouble with even her careless uncle, and furnished plentiful food for ill-natured tongues, she would have been more easy, less unhappy, more convinced. But Robert would not be made jealous, and his easy tranquil assumption of confident power, not laid aside even during the stolen interviews in which he bewildered her with his passionate protestations and caresses, sometimes nearly drove her mad. An instinct, which it had been well for her if she had heeded, told her that this man was not true to her. But she loved him madly. He had changed her whole nature, it seemed to her, in the few seldom-recurring moments in which she saw clearly into the past, and strained fearful eyes into the future; he had ruined the peace and happiness of her home, he had estranged her from her sister, he had taught her lessons of scorn and suspicion towards all her kind. But she loved him, him only in all the world.

Towards the close of the season, Haldane Carteret grew extremely impatient. He had been, he considered, quite an unreasonable time on duty, and he declared his intention of at once returning to the Deane. The men-servants would suffice for an escort for Mrs. Carteret and her nieces; or, if they did not like that arrangement, he was sure Meredith, who was coming down for the shooting at all events, would make it convenient to leave town a week or so sooner, and take care of them on the journey. No one had any objection to urge against this proposal; and Major Carteret took himself off, hardly more to his own satisfaction than to that of his wife, who declared herself worn out by his 'crossness,' and disgusted with his selfishness.

On the following evening Robert Meredith had a guest at his chambers, who, to judge by the moody and impatient expression of his host's countenance, was anything but welcome. Meredith had dined at Portman-square, where he had met George Ritherdon, to whom Miss Baldwin, with her simplest and yet most dignified air, had given, in her own and her uncle's name, an invitation to the Deane for the shooting season. This incident was highly displeasing to Meredith, who, distracted by an uneasy suspicion that his friend had found him out to a certain extent, desired nothing less than his presence during any part of the critical time which must elapse before he could make his *coup*. Robert had returned to his chambers in a sullen and exasperated temper, which was intensified by the spectacle which met his view. An old man, shabby of aspect, and anything but venerable in appearance or bearing—an old man with bleared watery eyes, bushy gray eyebrows, and dirty gray hair—was seated in an arm-chair by the open window, smoking a churchwarden pipe and drinking hot brandy-and-water. The mingled odours of tobacco and spirits perfumed the room after a fashion which harmonised ill with the sweet autumnal air and the flowers which adorned the sitting-room, in accordance with one of the owner's most harmless tastes.

'What, you here, Oakley!' said Meredith, in a tone which did not dissemble his disgust. 'What are you doing here? What has brought you up from Cheltenham?'

'Business,' replied the unvenerable visitor quietly, without rising or making any attempt at a salutation of his reluctant host.

'Business,' he repeated with an emphatic nod.

'With me?' Meredith threw his hat and gloves upon a table, and sat down, sullenly facing his visitor.

'With you. Look here, I'm tired of all this. You see, I am not so young as you are, and at my time of life I can't afford to play a waiting game. You can't, if you would, make it worth my while to do it; and as the case actually stands, you *don't* make it worth my while to play any game at all — of yours, I mean. Of course I should, in any case, play mine.'

'I don't understand you,' said Meredith, making a strong effort to keep his temper and speak with indifference. 'I have kept the terms I made with you to the letter. What do you mean by *your* game, as apart from mine?'

'Just this. I have no interest whatever

in your marrying this girl rather than in
any other man's marrying her. It does not
matter to me where my price comes from;
I'm sure of it from her husband, whoever
he may be, and I don't believe you're sure
that she *will* marry you. You have tried
to keep me dark, and in the dark, cunningly
enough; but I have found out more about
them than you think for, for all that; and
I know she has more than one string to her
bow, and at least one of them more profitable to play upon than you are. If you
can't persuade the girl to marry you before
she's of age, and raise money for me upon
her expectations, or if you can't in some
way make things more comfortable, I shall
try whether I cannot carry my information
to a better market. Indeed, I am so tired
of living respectably upon a pittance, paid
with a dreary exactitude which is distressingly like Somerset House, I have been seri-

ously contemplating an affecting visit to my relative Mrs. Carteret, and a family arrangement to buy me off at once at a long price.'

'And *my* knowledge of the affair; what do you make of *that*, in your rascally calculation?'

'Not quite so much as *you* make of it in *your* rascally calculation, my good friend; for it is not knowledge at all, it is only guesswork; and you have not an atom of proof without my evidence, which I am quite as willing to withhold as to give, for Mr. Trapbois' omnipotent motive—a consideration.'

For all answer, Robert Meredith rose, opened an iron safe let into the wall of the room, and hidden by a curtain—greedily followed the while by the old man's eyes, which watched for the gold he hoped he had extorted—and took out a red-leather pocket-book, with a clasp of brass wirework. He came up to the old man's side, and opening a page of the memorandum-book, pointed to an entry upon it.

'No evidence, I think you said. Not so fast, my faithful colleague. What is *that?*'

'Initials, a date,—a guess, Meredith, a mere surmise, not an atom of proof.'

'And this?' Robert Meredith took an oblong slip of paper out of a pocket in the book, and held it up to the old man's eyes. 'An attested copy of the marriage-register is evidence, I fancy.'

'Yes,' said Mr. Oakley reluctantly; 'that's evidence of one part of the story, to be sure; but not of the material part, the only part that's profitable to *you.* You can't do without me—you can't indeed; but I can do very well without you. You will save time and trouble by acknowledging the fact, and acting on it.'

'What the d—l do you want me to do?' said Meredith fiercely, as he threw the

pocket-book back into the safe and locked
the doors in a rage. 'I can't marry the girl
till she is of age. I tell you I am perfectly
sure of her. Do you think I am such a fool
as to allow any doubt to exist on that point?
But I don't choose to change my plans, and
I won't change them, let you threaten as
you will. You old idiot! you would ruin
yourself by thwarting me. You don't know
these people—*I do;* and you could as soon
induce them to join you in robbing a church
as to buy you off in the way you propose.
You had much better stick to the bargain
you've made, and have patience. I think if
I can find patience, *you* may.'

Mr. Oakley reflected for some minutes,
his bushy gray eyebrows meeting above his
frowning eyes. At last he said:

'Then I'll tell you what it is, Meredith.
You shall give me 20*l.* extra now, to-night,
and introduce me at once, to-morrow, to the

family, and we'll go on playing on the square again.'

'No,' said Meredith; 'it won't do. I can't give you 20*l.*; I can't spare the money. I'll give you 10*l.*, on condition you don't show yourself here until I send for you. And as to introducing you to the family just yet, it is out of the question. It would only embarrass our proceedings, and do you no good.'

'What do you mean?' said Oakley furiously. 'Why should you not introduce me to my own relative? I choose to partake of the advantages of her capital match. I intend to be Mrs. Carteret's guest at the Deane this autumn, whether the prospect be agreeable to you or not.'

Meredith smiled, a slow exasperating smile, carefully exaggerated into distinctness for the old man's dimmed vision, as he said:

'*I* could have no objection to do my good friend Mrs. Carteret the kindness of reuniting her with a long-severed member of her family, and to introduce you as a visitor at Portman-square, during the few days they will be in town, would not be any trouble to me; but as for your being invited to the Deane, the idea is *too* absurd.'

'And why?'

'Because Miss Baldwin, and not your relative, is the mistress of that very eligible mansion; because you are not the style of person Miss Baldwin admires; and because, you may take my word for it, you will never set your foot within those doors while the Deane belongs to Miss Baldwin.'

The old man's face turned a fiery red, and the angry colour showed itself under his thin gray hair.

'While the Deane belongs to Miss Baldwin!' he repeated low and slowly. 'Well, then, there's no use talking about it. Hand over the 10*l.*, and I'll be off.'

In a few minutes Robert Meredith was alone, and as he listened to Mr. Oakley's heavy tread upon the stairs, he muttered:

'It's a useful study, that of the ruling passions of one's fellow-creatures. An expert finds it tolerably easy to work them to his advantage. Avarice and pride! eh, Mr. Oakley? and pride the stronger of the two. You won't give me much more trouble. No danger of your being bribed to abstain from saying or doing anything that can harm Miss Baldwin.'

CHAPTER VIII.

THE MINE IS SPRUNG.

TIME sped on, and no fresh obstacle opposed itself to Robert Meredith's designs. His venerable colleague gave him no farther trouble. He had calculated with accuracy on Gertrude's nobility and delicacy of mind preventing her seeking to prejudice his friends in the household at the Deane against him, leading her to keep her promise of secrecy in its most perfect spirit. Thus, he pursued his design against her undisturbed, under her own roof, and with all the appearance of a good understanding existing between them.

Meredith was, however, mistaken in supposing that Gertrude was ignorant of her sister's attachment to him. She was much too keen-sighted where her affections were concerned to be deceived as to the state of Eleanor's mind, even had it not painfully revealed itself in the altered relations between them. She knew her sister's infatuation well, and she deplored it bitterly. The sorrow it caused her was all the more keen, because it was the first of her life in which she had not had recourse to Mr. Dugdale for advice, sympathy, and consolation. Now, she asked for none of these at his hands. She could not have claimed them without divulging the secret she had pledged herself to keep, and grieving the old man by changing his regard for the son of his dead friend into distrust and dislike. So Gertrude suffered in silence ; and as she became more and more isolated

—as she felt the sweet home ties relaxing daily—she clung all the more firmly to the hope, the conviction that George Ritherdon loved her ; though for some reason, which she was content to take on trust, to respect without understanding, he was resolved not to tell her so yet.

George Ritherdon passed three weeks, that autumn, at the Deane ; but Meredith avoided him—making an excuse for selecting the period of his visit for fulfilling another engagement. During those three weeks the regard and esteem of old Mr. Dugdale and George Ritherdon for each other so increased by intimacy, that Gertrude had the satisfaction of seeing them occupy the respective positions which she would most ardently have desired had her dearest hopes been realised. When George's visit had reached its conclusion, Mr. Dugdale took leave of him as he might have done of a son, and the young man left his old friend's rooms deeply affected. Gertrude was not much seen by the family that day, and it was understood Mr. Dugdale had requested her to pass the afternoon with him.

'Why does he say nothin', when any one that wasn't as blind as a bat could see he dotes on the ground she walks on?' asked Mr. Dugdale's faithful friend and confidante, Mrs. Doran, when they compared notes in the evening, after Gertrude had pleaded fatigue and left them.

'I don't know, indeed,' was Mr. Dugdale's answer. 'I suppose he thinks she has not had a fair chance of choosing yet.'

'Hasn't seen enough of grand young gentlemen just dyin' to put her money in their pockets, and spend it on other people, maybe!' said Mrs. Doran ironically. 'Bad luck to it, for money it's the curse of the world; for you don't know which does the most harm—too little of it, or too much! However, it's only waiting a bit, and they'll find each other out. Sure, he's a gentleman born and bred, and every inch of him, and made for her, if ever there was a match made in heaven.'

So Gertrude's best friends were silently waiting for the fulfilment of her hope. Mr. Dugdale had asked George Ritherdon to write to him frequently,— a request to which the young man had gratefully acceded; and his latest letter had informed Mr. Dugdale that he found himself obliged to leave London, for an indefinite period and at much inconvenience, owing to his mother's illness.

The time was now approaching when Eleanor should attain her majority, and Gertrude had resolved that the event should be celebrated with all the distinction which had attended her own.

To Eleanor and to Mrs. Carteret the
birthday-fête had the surpassing attraction
of a charming entertainment, rendered still
more delightful by the presence of the
lover of the one and the particular friend
of the other. To Gertrude, though she
strove to be bright and gay, and though
she sought by every means in her power
to evince her affection for the sister who
turned away with steady coldness from
all her advances, the occasion was a melancholy one. It furnished a sad contrast
to the fête which had welcomed her own
coming of age in every respect,—above all,
in that one which had become most important to her: George was not present.

Robert Meredith caused his manner to
be remarked on this occasion by more than
one of the guests at the Deane. To Miss
Baldwin he was scrupulously but distantly
polite; with Mrs. Carteret he assumed a

tone of intimacy which she seconded to the full; but to Eleanor he bore himself like an acknowledged and triumphant lover. Every one saw this, including Mr. Dugdale, during his brief visit to the scene of the festivities, and Haldane Carteret, not remarkable for quickness of observation. The fact made both these observers uneasy, but they did not make any comment to one another upon their suspicions.

The sisters, who had each been dancing nearly all night, did not meet on the conclusion of the ball. The old familiar habit of a long talk, in one of their respective dressing-rooms, after all the household had retired, had long been abandoned; and when, on this occasion, Gertrude—resolved to make an effort to break through the barrier so silently but effectually reared between them—went to her sister's room, she found the door locked, and though she heard Eleanor moving about, no answer to her petition for admittance was returned. Full of care and foreboding, Gertrude returned to her room, and it was broad day before she forgot her grief, and the presentiment of evil which accompanied it, in sleep.

The ladies did not appear at breakfast the next morning, and the party consisted only of Major Carteret, Robert Meredith, and two harmless individuals who were staying in the house, and in no way remarkable or important. On the conclusion of the meal Robert Meredith requested Major Carteret to accord him an interview, which the latter agreed to do with some hesitation. They adjourned to the library, and there Meredith, with no circumlocution, and in a plain and business-like manner, informed Major Carteret that he had proposed to his niece Eleanor Baldwin, been accepted by her, and that she had requested him to communicate the fact to Major Carteret.

Eleanor's uncle received the intelligence with awkwardness rather than with actual disapprobation, and acquitted himself not very well in replying. Something of un-pleasantly - felt power in Meredith's tone jarred upon him as he used a perfectly discreet formula of words in making the announcement. Haldane Carteret did not dislike or distrust Meredith, and he was not an interested man. He had married for love himself, and he knew his niece had sufficient fortune to deprive her con-duct of imprudence, if she chose to do the same. It was not fair to take it for granted that Meredith was not attached to Eleanor, that he was actuated by in-terested motives ; and yet Haldane Car-teret, an honest man, if not bright, felt that all was not straightforward and simple feeling in this matter. He said something about disparity of age; then admitted that, in referring Meredith to him, his niece had merely treated him with dutiful courtesy, as his guardianship and authority had terminated ; and finally, on being pressed by Meredith, said he perceived no objection, beyond the evident one that his niece might have looked for more decided worldly advantages in her marriage, and that he thought the proceeding had been somewhat too precipitate for the best interests of both. All this Haldane Carteret said, because his native honesty obliged him to say it; but heartily wishing he could bring the interview to a close, or hand Meredith over to his wife, who would probably be delighted.

Meredith received Major Carteret's remarks with calm politeness, but hardly

thought it necessary to combat them. He
could not see the disparity in age in any
serious light, and he ventured to assure
his Eleanor's uncle he and she had understood one another for some time ; there
was no real precipitation in the matter.
As for the advantages which such a marriage secured to him, he was most ready
to acknowledge them, and to admit their
effect on the general estimate of his motives, but he did not mind .that. Secure
against an unkind interpretation by Eleanor and her relatives, he was indifferent
to any other opinion. He flattered himself Mrs. Carteret would learn the news
with satisfaction. This was ground on
which Major Carteret could meet him with
cordial assent ; and he got over his diffi-
culties by referring the happy lover to
Mrs. Carteret; and having summoned her
to the library to receive Meredith's com-

munication from himself, he left them together.

Mrs. Carteret was expansively and en-
thusiastically delighted. She declared she
felt herself quite a girl again in contemplating the happiness of her beloved niece
and her old friend ; and it may be assumed that Robert Meredith had evinced
very nice tact and discretion in the method by which he conveyed the information
to her.

It was no small portion of the suffering which Gertrude Baldwin had to un-
dergo at this time, that she heard the
news of her sister's engagement—not from
Eleanor herself, not in any kindly sisterly
conference, but from Mrs. Carteret, whose
light gleeful manner of imparting the information to Gertrude was far from conveying any sense of its importance to the
agitated girl ; and who filled up the mea-

sure of her congratulations to everybody
concerned, by remarking that in 'poor
dear Eleanor's invidious position, it was
most desirable that she should marry
early, and before Gerty had made her
choice.' This speech chilled Gertrude into
silence, and she left her aunt—having uttered only a few commonplace words —
with the well - founded conviction that
Eleanor would believe her either envious,
indifferent, or prejudiced against her and
Meredith. Gertrude was quite alone in
her distress of mind, as she purposely
avoided Mr. Dugdale—being unwilling to
awaken a suspicion in his mind of its cause
— and Mrs. Doran, who she instinctively
knew would penetrate and share her feelings.

In the course of the day both those
members of the family were made aware
of Eleanor's engagement. Old Mr. Dug-

dale took the intimation very calmly, as
it was his wont to take all things now,
since he had ceased to feel keenly save
where Gertrude was concerned. Mrs. Doran heard it, with a sad foreboding heart
and a gloomy face. She had never liked,
she had never trusted Robert Meredith ;
and she could not forget that the man her
dear dead mistress's daughter was about
to marry was the same who, as a boy, had
hated Margaret.

Robert Meredith and Gertrude did not
meet alone. They mutually and successfully avoided each other, and the elder
sister was pointedly excluded by Eleanor
and Mrs. Carteret from all the discussions
which ensued relative to the arrangements
for the marriage, which was to take place
soon. Gertrude heard that her aunt and
her sister purposed to go to London, to
purchase Eleanor's *trousseau*, to select

Eleanor's house, without a word of comment. But when something was said about
the marriage taking place in London, she
interposed, and in her customary sweet
and yet dignified way remonstrated. Eleanor, she said, ought to leave no house for
a husband's, but her own.

'Mine!' said Eleanor. 'I presume you
mean yours—you are talking of the Deane.'

'I am talking of our mutual home,
Eleanor, where once no such evil thing as
a divided interest ever had a place.—Uncle,'
—here she turned to Major Carteret, and
laid her hand impressively upon his arm,
—'speak for me in this. Tell Eleanor I
am right, and that our parents—I, at least,
have never felt their loss so bitterly before—would have had it so.'

'I'm sure I don't know what to say,'
replied Haldane Carteret forlornly. 'I
can't conceive what has come between you

two girls; but I must say I do think Gerty
is in the right in this instance. — Lucy,
my dear, the wedding must be at . the
Deane.'

So that was settled; and afterwards,
until Eleanor and Mrs. Carteret, accompanied by Robert Meredith, went to London, things were better between the sisters.
There was not, indeed, any renewal of the
intimate affection, the unrestrained cordi-
ality of other times; and Gertrude felt
mournfully that a complete restoration
could never be—the constant interposition
of Meredith would render that impossible.
Under ordinary circumstances, the marriage of one by involving separation from
the other must have loosened the old bonds;
but this marriage was indeed fatal. They
were young girls, however, and the evil
influence which had come between them
had not yet completely done its work, had

not spoiled all their common interest in
the topics which fittingly engage the minds
of young girls. Gertrude strove to forget
her own wounded feelings, to conquer her
apprehensions, and to disarm the jealous
reticence of her sister by frank interest
and generous zeal. She succeeded to some
extent, and the interval between the declaration of the engagement and the departure of Mrs. Carteret and Eleanor was the
happiest time, so far as she was individually concerned, that Gertrude had known
since the first painful consciousness of di-
vision had come between the sisters.

Everything went on quietly on the surface of life at the Deane when Eleanor
and her aunt had left home. Mr. Dugdale was a little more feeble, perhaps; his
daily airing upon the terrace was shorter,
his period of seclusion in his own rooms
was lengthened; but he was very cheerful,

and seemed to desire Gertrude's presence more constantly than ever.

The visit to London was as prosperous as its purpose was pleasant. Mrs. Carteret's letters were quite exultant. Never had she enjoyed herself more, she flattered herself Eleanor's *trousseau* was unimpeachable, and Robert Meredith was the most devoted of lovers and the most delightful of men. She had had an agreeable surprise, too, since she had been in London. She fancied she had chanced to mention to Gertrude that a distant relative of hers, whom she had only seen as a very young child—a Mr. Oakley—had gone out to Australia, and, it had happened oddly enough, had there known Robert Meredith's father and their beloved Margaret's first husband; indeed, he had known Gertrude's dear mother herself. This gentleman—a fine venerable old man, 'quite a Rembrandt's head,

indeed,' Mrs. Carteret added—was now in
London, having made an honourable independence; and he naturally wished to find
friends and a little social intercourse among
such of his relatives as were still living.
Mr. Meredith had brought him to see her,
and the dear old gentleman had been much
gratified and deeply affected by the meeting. Mrs. Carteret went on to say that,
knowing dear Gertrude's invariable kindness and wish to please everybody, and
also taking into consideration her characteristic respect for old age combined with
virtue and respectability,—so remarkably
displayed in the case of their dear Mr.
Dugdale, — she had ventured to promise
Mr. Oakley a welcome to the Deane, on
behalf of Miss Baldwin, on the approaching auspicious occasion.

To this letter Gertrude replied promptly,
expressing her pleasure at having it in her

power to gratify Mrs. Carteret, and en-
closing a cordially-worded invitation to the
Deane to the venerable old gentleman with
the Rembrandt head; who received it with
a chuckle, and a muttered commendation
of the long-sightedness which had made
Robert Meredith defer his introduction to
Miss Baldwin until the present truly convenient season.

On her side, Gertrude was making preparations on a splendid scale for the cele-
bration of her sister's marriage in her
ancestral home. Nothing that affection
and generosity could suggest was neglected
by the young heiress, whose own tastes
were of the simplest order, to gratify those
of Eleanor. She lavished gifts upon her
with an unsparing hand, and, indeed, valued
her wealth chiefly because it enabled her
to obey the dictates of a most generous
nature.

Mrs. Carteret and Eleanor returned to
the Deane, attended by Mr. Oakley. Robert Meredith was to follow the day before that fixed for the wedding. The old
gentleman did not impress Gertrude particularly as being venerable, as distinguished
from old, in either person or manner; and
she quickly perceived that Mrs. Carteret
was aware and ashamed of his underbred
presuming manners. This perception, however, was only another motive to induce
Gertrude to treat him with the utmost
courtesy and consideration. She must
shield her aunt from any unpleasantness
which might arise in consequence of her
relative's evident unfitness for the society
into which she had brought him. At all
events, it would only be putting up with
him for a short time, and he certainly could
do no harm. So Gertrude was perseveringly
kind and gentle to Mr. Oakley, and actually

so far impressed the old gentleman favourably, that he believed Robert Meredith to have lied in imputing disdainful pride to her, and almost regretted the part he had undertaken to play. There was no help for it now, however; he might as well profit by the transaction, which it was altogether too late to avert. Thus did the faint scruples called into existence in Mr. Oakley's breast, by the unassuming and graceful goodness of the girl he had undertaken to injure, fall flat before the strength of interested rascality.

The wedding of Eleanor Meriton Baldwin presented a striking contrast to that of her mother, which had excited so much contemptuous comment among the 'neighbours' in the old, old times at Chayleigh. People of rank, wealth, and fashion assembled in gorgeous attire to behold the ceremonial, which was rendered as stately

and imposing as possible. The dress of the
bride was magnificent, and her beauty was
the theme of every tongue. The bridegroom was rather less insignificant than
the bridegroom generally is, and looked
happy and contented; as well he might
look, the people said, getting such a fortune. Miss Baldwin's own husband would
not be so lucky in some respects; for this
gentleman might do as he pleased with
Miss Nelly's money—she *would* have it so,
and she could leave him the whole of it—
whereas in Miss Baldwin's case it would
be different.

The wedding-guests were splendidly
entertained; all agreed that the whole affair had been exceptionally prosperous.
The leave-taking between the sisters was
not witnessed by any intrusive eyes; and
in the final hurry and confusion no one
noticed that Robert Meredith did not

shake hands with Miss Baldwin, that he
spoke no word to her. Gertrude noticed
the omission, and with pain. It was over
now, and she would fain have made the
best of it — have been friends with her
sister's husband, if he would have allowed
her to be so. That he should have been
thus vindictive on his wedding-day, that
he should have had place in his heart for
any thought of anger or ill-will, boded
evil to Eleanor's peace, her sister thought.
But it never occurred to her to fear that
it might also bode evil to her own, otherwise than through that sister whom she
loved.

In Scottish fashion a ball wound up the
festivities of the Deane, and proved, in its
turn, a successful entertainment. Miss
Baldwin, indeed, looked tired and pale;
but that was only natural, after so much
excitement and the parting with her sis-

ter. The dreamy look that came over her at times was easily explicable, without any one's being likely to divine that the absence of one figure from that brilliant crowd had anything to do with its origin. And yet, as the hours wore on, Gertrude forgot the fresh pang the day had brought her—forgot Meredith and her forebodings, forgot all save George Ritherdon and that he was not there.

Three weeks had elapsed since Eleanor Baldwin's marriage. Mrs. Carteret had received two short letters from the bride, but Mrs. Meredith had not written to her sister. Mr. Oakley was still at the Deane, where his presence had become exceedingly unpleasant not only to Miss Baldwin, but to Major and Mrs. Carteret, to whom he had dropped one or two hints relative to Meredith's character and probable treatment of Eleanor, which had made them vaguely, though unavowedly, uncomfortable. Gertrude was keenly distressed, and had found it impossible to keep the knowledge of her trouble and its cause from Mr. Dugdale. Some unnamed undefinable evil seemed to be brooding over the Deane. It was not known exactly where the newly-married pair were. Eleanor had given no address in her last letter, and Gertrude and Mrs. Carteret (the latter most unwillingly) admitted that it seemed constrained and strangely reticent.

The fourth week had begun, when one morning, as the family party were dispersing after breakfast, a servant announced the arrival of a gentleman from London, who desired to see Miss Baldwin on urgent business. He placed a card in his mistress's hand as he delivered the message.

'Mr. Sankey!' read Gertrude aloud; 'I don't know the name. What can his business be with me?'

'*I* know the name,' said Mr. Oakley hurriedly, 'and I fear I know the business he comes on too. Meredith has sent him. —Major Carteret, you had better see this gentleman first — you had, indeed. Miss Baldwin cannot be spared *much;* but do you come with, me and see him, and let us spare her all we can.'

CHAPTER IX.

THE RIGHTING OF THE WRONG.

SOME years have passed since the blow fell on Gertrude Baldwin which deprived her of wealth and station, which struck away from her her home, and left her to face the curiosity, the ill-will, the evil report of the world which had envied and flattered her, as best she might. The story of the interval does not take long in the telling, and, considering its import to so many, has but few salient points.

No resistance was made by Gertrude or counselled by her advisers; no resistance to the hard cold terms of Robert Meredith's claim on his wife's behalf. It was all true: Gertrude was an illegitimate child and

Eleanor the rightful heir. The proofs—consisting of Mr. Oakley's evidence concerning Godfrey Hungerford's death, and the attested certificate of the date of that occurrence, and the testimony of the certificate of the second marriage ceremony performed between Mr. Baldwin and Margaret — were as simple as they were indisputable, and Gertrude made unqualified submission at once.

She suffered, no doubt, very keenly, but much less than her friends Mr. Dugdale and Rose Doran suffered for her. So much was made plain to her, so much was cleared-up to her now. She knew now why it was her father had left her nothing by his will; she understood now from what solicitude it had arisen that he and her aunt, whose loving care she remembered so well, had bequeathed everything within their power to Eleanor. Thus they had endeavoured to atone for the

unconscious unintentional wrong done to the
legitimate daughter and heiress. And all
their efforts, all their care, had failed; the
invincible inexorable truth had come to
light, and the result of all these efforts was
that Eleanor had everything—yes, everything. The young girl who had risen that
morning absolute mistress of the splendid
house and the broad acres of the Deane,
and the large fortune which could so fittingly maintain them, stood in that stately
house the same night a penniless dependent
on the sister who had placed herself and all
she possessed in the power of Gertrude's
only enemy.

It was long before Miss Baldwin, or
indeed any of the party, realised this—long
before the full extent of the truth presented
itself to their minds; but when it came, it
came with terrible conviction and conclu-
siveness. There was nothing for Gertrude.

Her father's loving care had indeed been her undoing. The situation was a dreadful one, escape from it impossible. Robert Meredith had no longer anything to gain by either dissimulation or temporising ; on the contrary, he now felt it to be his interest that every one concerned should be cured of all their illusions concerning him as soon and as effectually as possible, and should arrive at a clear comprehension of his powers, motives, and intentions. He assumed at once the name that his marriage with the heiress of Mr. Meriton Baldwin imposed upon him; and his letter to Haldane Carteret was simply a reference to the bearer as qualified to give all needful explanations and proofs, and in the event, which he took for granted, of the young lady known as Miss Baldwin not disputing the facts, he begged it might be understood that she could be suffered to remain at the

Deane only a very short time. He hoped
no farther communication on this subject
might be required. The young lady would
best consult her own interest by abstaining
from making any such communication necessary.

It is unnecessary to dwell on this portion of the trial appointed to Gertrude.
Its bitterness came from Eleanor, not from
her triumphant enemy. Her sister made
no sign—not a word of kindness, of sympathy, of regret came from her whose life
had been almost identical with that of Gertrude for so many years. Even Mrs. Carteret—who, the first shock and surprise
over, was characteristically disposed to keep
on good terms with the new Mr. Meriton
Baldwin, and in reality an extreme partisan, endeavoured to get credit for im-
partial fairness, and a 'no business of mine'
bearing—even Mrs. Carteret was indignant

with Eleanor.   Her shallow nature did not comprehend the growth and force of such evil feelings as she had nurtured in the mind of her niece.   Gertrude suffered fearfully, but anger had little share in her pain. A deadly fear for her sister possessed her; a fear which suggested itself speedily, when she found that Eleanor made no sign, and which grew into conviction under the influence of Rose Doran's manifest belief in its reason and validity.   Eleanor's silence was her husband's doing; she was under his influence and dominion, she was afraid of him.   When Gertrude, who had striven to hide her feelings on this point from Mr. Dugdale, could not hide them from Rose Doran, that faithful friend said sadly,

'It's true for you, Miss Gerty; she's in the grip of a bad man, my poor child, and she's not to be blamed.'

Then Gertrude, in the depth of her love

and pity for her sister, forgave her freely, and never did blame her more, but mourned for her, as she might have done had she been dead and laid beside their mother beneath the great yew-tree, only more bitterly. All it is necessary to record here is, that Eleanor's silence remained unbroken —unbroken, when her sister, with Mr. Dugdale and Mrs. Doran left the Deane for ever, turning away from all the associations and surroundings which had been mutually dear to them—unbroken, when some time after Gertrude wrote to her to tell her that she was well and happy, and more than reconciled to all that had befallen her, except only her alienation from her sister's heart.

Much time had now gone over, and Eleanor's silence still remained unbroken. There was absolutely no communication between the sisters. Major and Mrs. Car-

teret were living at Chayleigh, in a style
which at first Lucy had found it not easy
to adopt after the pleasant places of the
Deane. But she had hit upon a consolation
which, if imaginary, was likewise immense;
this was the notion of independence. To
be her own mistress, the mistress of her
own house, her own servants, and her own
time was discovered by Mrs. Carteret to
be a blissful state of things. Besides this
consolation, she had soon 'brought round'
Major Carteret to an acquiescent form of
mind respecting the state of things at the
Deane, and they made frequent visits there;
but not even in this indirect way was the
separation between the sisters modified.
Mrs. Carteret was given to understand on
the first occasion of her meeting Mr. and
Mrs. Meredith Baldwin—and a very awk-
ward meeting it was—that it would be for
her own interest to abstain from speaking

of Gertrude to Eleanor, and, indeed, that her retaining the valuable privilege of an *entrée* at the Deane was contingent on her strict obedience to this hint. Mrs. Carteret proved worthy of her old friend's confidence; and the former life at the Deane might never have had existence for any reminiscence of it that was to be traced now.

The intelligence which reached Gertrude of her sister through her uncle and aunt was too vague to satisfy her. Eleanor was very popular, very much admired; Eleanor's entertainments were splendid; and Mrs. Carteret felt convinced she and Meredith Baldwin lived fully up to their income, large as it was. She really could not say whether Eleanor was *happy*, according to dear Gertrude's strange exaggerated notions. She had at least everything which ought to make her so, and she was always

in very high spirits. She was rather restless and fond of change, and no doubt
Meredith *was* a good deal away from her;
and then poor dear Eleanor had always
had a strong dash of jealousy in her disposition, and she never was remarkably
reasonable. No doubt she did occasionally
make herself unpleasant and ridiculous if
her husband stayed away when she thought
he ought to be with her; but she got over
it again, and it did not signify. As to
Meredith's ill-treating Eleanor, Mrs. Carteret begged Gertrude not to be so silly
as to believe anything of the kind, if such
ill-natured reports should reach her. Why,
everybody knew Meredith was no fool; and
if Eleanor (who was very delicate—and no
wonder, considering her restless racketing)
did not make a will in his favour, he
would have nothing at all in case of her
death. There was no heir to the Deane—

two infants had been born, but each had
lived only a few hours—and Mrs. Carteret
knew positively that Eleanor had made no
will. Meredith was not likely (supposing
him to have no better motive—which Mrs.
Carteret, though her tone had become
greatly modified of late in speaking of her
quondam admirer, could not endure to suppose) to endanger his chance of future
independent wealth by ill-treating the person who could confer it on him.

This was poor comfort; but it was all
Gertrude could get, and she was forced to
be content with it. The old life at the Deane
had faded away; no change could bring
her back the past; she never could have
any interest in it. She sometimes speculated upon whether it would add to her
grief, if her sister died, to think of her
father's property, her own old home, in the
possession of total strangers. She had

hardly ever heard anything of the next
heir—a bachelor, already a rich man, living
in England. This gentleman's name was
Mordaunt, and he had a younger brother,
who had assumed another name on his
marriage, and to whose children the Deane,
failing direct heirs of Eleanor, would de-
scend. The sisters knew nothing more of
these distant connections, nor had there
ever been any acquaintance between them
and Fitzwilliam Baldwin.

Though Gertrude sometimes pondered
on these things it must not be supposed
that she brooded on them, or that the irre-
vocable past filled an undue place in her
practical and useful life. The misfortune
which had befallen her had from the first
its alleviations; and there came a day when
Gertrude would have eagerly denied that
it was a misfortune at all—a day when she
would have declared it was the source of

all her happiness, the providential solution of every doubt and difficulty which had beset her path. What that day was the reader is soon to know.

The first act of Mr. Dugdale when the truth was made known to him—when he clearly understood that once more the foreboding of the woman he had loved and mourned with such matchless and abiding constancy had been fulfilled so many years after its shadow had darkened her day—was to declare his intention of immediately leaving the Deane, and forming a new home for Gertrude. How devoutly he thanked God then for the life at whose duration he had been sometimes tempted to murmur, the length of days which had enabled him to profit by the impulse which had prompted him to decline to add to the ruin which, in their blindness, they had all accumulated to heap in Gertrude's path ! When he explained this to her, and made her see how her father and mother had loved her, great peace came to Gertrude, and much happiness in the perfect confidence between her and her aged friend, owning no exception now. In his zeal for Margaret's child, Mr. Dugdale seemed to find strength which had not been his for years. He bore the journey to the neighbourhood of London, whither Mrs. Doran had preceded them for the purpose of engaging a house for them, well; and he settled into his new home as readily as Gertrude did.

In a neat small house in a western suburb of London, George Ritherdon found Mr. Dugdale and her whom he had last seen in all the lustre of wealth and station, when he returned from the long absence which had been occasioned by his mother's illness and subsequent death. George was perfectly conscious that neither his voice nor his manner, when he was introduced by the faithful Rose with manifest satisfaction, conveyed the impression which might have been considered suitable to the occasion, whether regarded from their point of view or from his. He knew his eyes were bright and his cheek flushed; he knew his voice was thrilling with pleasure, with happiness, with hope; and he abandoned any attempt to express a sadness he did not feel, to affect to grieve for a change in Gertrude's circumstances and position which rendered him exquisitely happy, and for which he, though by no means a presumptuous man, felt an inward irresistible conviction he should be able to console her.

In less than a year from the falling of the long-planned blow on Gertrude Baldwin's defenceless head, the day before al-

luded to had dawned upon her—the day on
which she recognised the seemingly insur-
mountable misfortune of her life as its
greatest blessing and the source of all its
happiness. It was her wedding-day. There
was no need for waiting longer for equality
in their fortunes; there was no need to
think of what the world might say of
George or of her. The world she had lived
in had ceased to remember and to talk of
her; the world he lived in would respect
him, as it had ever done, and welcome her.
Theirs was a quiet happy courtship, a
peaceful hopeful time, blessed with their
old friend's earnest approval and loving
presence. A rational prospect of the best
kind of content this world can give was
opening before them—a prospect of neither
poverty nor riches, of no distinction in mere
name—the meaningless legacy of others—
but of a position to be worthily won. Mu-

tual love, confidence, and respect, and such experience of life as, leaving them the power of enjoying its good, should save them from its illusions—such was the dowry with which these two began their married life.

Major and Mrs. Carteret attended the quiet wedding, at which they and two friends of George Ritherdon's were the only guests. Gertrude had hoped that Mrs. Carteret would have been the bearer to her of some communication from her sister, that the barrier, which she felt no doubt had been interposed by Meredith's authority, would on this occasion be broken down. But Eleanor still made no sign; and Mrs. Carteret could tell Gertrude no more than that Eleanor had heard the news of her sister's intended marriage with agitation, but in silence, and that she was then in London, *en route* for the Continent, where she was to pass the winter. This was a cloud; but it was the only one upon the brightness of Gertrude's wedding-day, and it soon passed over. It had quite passed when the bride and bridegroom were bidding farewell to Mr. Dugdale, before they went away on their brief wedding-trip. It was to be very brief; for they would not leave him alone for any length of time; and in the mean time Mr. Dugdale was to remove into the larger house in the same neighbourhood which was to be the home of George and Gertrude.

The farewell words had been spoken, and Gertrude had risen from her kneeling position beside the old man's chair, when the servant entered and handed Gertrude a parcel addressed to her by the name not three hours old, addressed to her in Eleanor's hand. She broke the seal, and the contents proved to be a flat case containing a suit of beautiful pearls. A scrap of paper lay among the jewels. Gertrude seized it eagerly and read:

'*Wear these, darling, for the sake of old times, and of me. Forgive me, and make your husband forgive me, and love me a little even yet and after all, as I love you forever and better than all.*'

As Gertrude's tears fell fast upon the precious words, and George and Mr. Dugdale looked at her, distressed and yet glad, Rose Doran came to her side, and said, while she dried her eyes as if she were still the child she had nursed:

'There, there, alanna, didn't I tell you it wasn't *her* fault at all, but *his?* and now you see for yourself it's true, and you'll go away with an easier mind. And, mark my words, it's coming right—it's coming right by degrees, and it will all come right in the end.'

Mr. Dugdale still kept late hours, as he

had done all his life. Mrs. Doran left him
at the usual hour in more than his accustomed spirits, and not apparently fatigued
by the unusual emotion of the day. When
he was alone, the old man passed some
time in reading; then he closed his book
and gave himself up to thought. His
thoughts were seemingly very peaceful,
and not sad; for there was a calm and patient smile upon the worn face, to which
old age had brought a serene dignity. His
large deeply-cushioned arm-chair moved
easily upon its castors, and, after a period
of profound stillness, he rolled himself in
the chair towards a writing-table, on which
a lamp was burning. He unlocked a deep
drawer, the lowest of a set on his right-
hand, and took out two objects. One was
his will, which he spread out upon the
table and read attentively. Then mutter-
ing to himself, 'A few kind words to Nelly,

—God help her, poor child!' he wrote half-a-dozen lines on the reverse of one of the pages of the document, and appended his initials in a clear and steady hand. This done, he replaced the paper in the drawer, and turned his attention to the other object he had taken out.

It was the portrait of Margaret, in its beautiful setting of passion-flowers in jeweller's work of enamel and gold. There was reverential tenderness in the old man's touch as he placed the picture upright before him, opened the screens of golden filigree, and 'fell to such perusal' of it as had been familiar to him since the coffin-lid had closed over the face it feebly shadowed forth. The minutes fled by as he gazed upon the likeness of the beautiful spiritual face which had gone down to the grave in untouched loveliness; and a glass upon his dressing-table alongside reflected his bowed head, sunken features, bent shadowy figure, and thin gray hair. Now and then a few unconnected murmurs escaped his lips, but rarely; while his gaze remained fixed, and a solemn peacefulness spread over his face.

'The same eyes in heaven,' he whispered, 'the same smile. How many years have I looked for them, and longed for them—how many, many years! I shall go to *her;* but she has not been waiting and watching for *me.* No, no; heaven has been full enough to her all this time with *him* there.'

He changed the position of the picture slightly, and leaned his head back against the cushion in his chair, looking at the face from a greater distance; then stretched out his folded hands and rested them upon the table.

'A long, long time—but nearly over, I

think — and I have not murmured over-
much, for your sake, Margaret. But now,
now I think I may make the *Nunc dimittis*
my evensong.'

A little longer the old man's gaze remained fixed upon the picture; and then
his form settled down amid the cushions,
his hands fell gently from the edge of the
table upon his knees, and his eyes closed
softly. Through the hours of the night
the lamp burned, and lighted up the picture
with its golden trellised covers unclosed,
and lighted up the old man's serene face.
But with the morning the flame in the
lamp flickered and died, and the sunshine
came in, and gleamed upon the walls and
the floor. Voices and footsteps stirred in the
house, and soon Mrs. Doran came to Mr.
Dugdale's room, as she did every morning.
Then she knew, when she looked at the old
man and touched his passive hands, still

clasped and resting on his knee,—so gentle
had been the parting between the body and
the spirit,—that his sleep was never to know
waking until the resurrection morning.

The blinds are closely drawn in Gertrude Ritherdon's house, and she sits alone,
dressed in deep mourning. There is a touch
of sadness upon her beauty; but she is
more beautiful than she was in her girlhood, and for all the sorrow in her face to-
day, one can see she is a happy woman.
She is so. A happy wife, loved, trusted,
honoured; her husband's companion and
his friend. A proud and happy mother
too, untroubled, when she watches her
boy's baby glee and hears his laughter,
with any remembrance of a great inherit-
ance which was once to have been the
birthright of her first-born son. A happy
woman in her house, and popular with her

friends; one whose life is full of blessings
and void of bitterness. It is not for her
faithful old friend Gertrude Ritherdon wears
mourning to-day. That wound has long
been healed, and she and her husband have
none but sunny happy thoughts of him.
Death has come nearer to Gertrude this
time even than he came when Mr. Dugdale
answered his summons — they have received formal notice of Eleanor's decease.
The event has been long looked for, and
Gertrude has well known that life has had
nothing desirable in it for Eleanor. The
sisters have never met, and of late Eleanor
has lived abroad altogether, her husband
being rarely with her; but Gertrude knows
that her sister's former feelings have long
ago returned, and there is sorrow, but not
anguish, in this definitive earthly parting.

George Ritherdon has been summoned
to Naples, where Eleanor Baldwin died, by

Major Carteret, and Gertrude is now expecting his return. Her thoughts have been busy with the past; and when they have rested upon Robert Meredith, it has been without any anger for herself, but with some wonder as to how he will take the passing away to a stranger of all the wealth and luxury he bought at such a price, and enjoyed for so comparatively short a time. He will be a rich man, no doubt, with all Eleanor had to bestow on him; but he will have to see a stranger in the place he filled so pompously, and to feel himself once more a person of no importance. For Eleanor has died childless, and the Deane passes away to the eldest son of the late brother of that Mr. Mordaunt who was the next in the entail, and who, strange to say, died only two days before the death of Mrs. Meredith Baldwin occurred. Gertrude has heard this vaguely, in the hurry of George's

departure, and during the first bewilder-
ment which death brings with it.

A carriage stops, and Gertrude lifts the
end of a blind and looks out. Two gentlemen enter the house, and in a few seconds
she is clasped in her husband's arms, and
sees, standing behind him, her uncle, Major
Carteret. She greets him affectionately,
and then loses her composure and bursts
into tears. The two men allow her to give
vent to her feelings without remonstrance,
and when she is again calm, they talk a
little of their journey, and then approach
the subject of Eleanor's death. Gertrude
knows the particulars of the event, and
they go on to speak of the will.

'I thought it better to tell you than to
write about it,' says George. 'You must
prepare for a surprise, Gertrude. Eleanor
has left her entire fortune — it is much
wasted, but still large—to you.'

'To me!' exclaimed Gertrude, 'to me! And what has she left to Meredith?'

'Nothing,' replied Major Carteret. 'Precisely what he deserved. She makes no mention of him, his name does not occur in the will. She probably explains her motives and tells the sad story of her life in a letter which she left directed to me, that I may give it unopened into your hands. You shall have it, but hear first what we have to tell you. She has left you everything in her power to bequeath, and left it all at your absolute disposal.'

Gertrude seemed stupefied. At length she said slowly:

'What must he feel? 'What did he say?'

'I don't know what he felt,' replied Major Carteret. 'What he said quickly deprived me of all inclination to pity him, the scoundrel! I hope we have all heard and seen the last of him. His worthy as-

sociate, Oakley, made me understand his
character long ago; but while poor Nelly
lived it would have served no purpose to
resent it, and we had nothing to gain by
exposing him. Now it turns out she has
avenged herself and us all, and we can
afford to dismiss him from our minds. You
must allow me to congratulate you, Gertrude, on poor Nelly's handsome legacy,
and then on something much more important still.'

Gertrude looked from her husband to
her uncle nervously, and her lips trembled.

'What is it? I can't bear much more.'

George put his arm firmly round her,
and placing her on a sofa, took his place by
her side. At this moment Mrs. Doran came
quietly into the room and approached the
group. Haldane made her a sign to be
silent, while George spoke to his wife:

'While I was staying at the Deane,

when I first went there for your birthday,
Gertrude, my mother wrote to me, and
told me it was a curious circumstance that
I should be a visitor at Miss Baldwin's
house. Why? Can you guess?'

Gertrude silently shook her head.

' Because, as I then learned for the first
time, my father's old bachelor brother, Mr.
Mordaunt, was in the entail of the Deane,
and in the very improbable event of there
being no direct heir, that which has come
to pass might come to pass. Do you understand what has happened now, my darling?'

' No,' stammered Gertrude; 'I—I do not.'

' This is what has happened: my uncle,
Mr. Mordaunt, is dead. I am his heir. My
father took my mother's name in consequence of a family quarrel about his marriage, and, as you know, he died some years
ago. I am the next in the entail, and Elea-

nor's dying without a child, makes me the possessor of the Deane. You now know why I did not ask you to be my wife when I believed you to be the lawful owner of the property; you now know how doubly joyfully I made you my wife when you lost it. Gertrude, my darling, I think you will prize your old name and your old home more than ever now that it is your husband who gives them back to you.'

'I said it would all come right, Miss Gerty, didn't I, alanna?' exclaimed Rose Doran, as she in her turn caught Gertrude in her strong arms, and rocked her to and fro like an infant. 'But I never thought it could come *so* right. Honest people and rogues have got their due in *this* world, once in a way, anyhow.'

THE END.

LONDON : ROBSON AND SONS, PRINTERS, PANCRAS ROAD, N.W.